# Gravity's Volkswagen

Also by GEOFF NICHOLSON

# GRAVITY'S VOLKSWAGEN

## Geoff Nicholson

Harbour

First published in paperback original by Harbour in 2009
Harbour Books Ltd, 20 Castlegate, York YO1 9RP
publicity@harbourbooks.co.uk
www.harbourbooks.co.uk

UK and Ireland sales by Signature
20 Castlegate, York YO1 9RP
Tel 01904 633633    Fax 01904 675445
sales@signaturebooks.co.uk

A catalogue record for this book is
available from the British Library.

ISBN    978 1 905128 14 3

Typeset by Antony Gray
Printed and bound in Finland by WS Bookwell

# EXTRACTS
## (supplied by a sub-sub-librarian)

One particular swindle perpetrated by Hitler on the German workers deserves passing mention. This had to do with the Volkswagen (the 'People's Car') – a brainstorm of the Führer himself. Every German, or at least every German workman, he said, should own an automobile, just as in the United States . . .

Alas for the worker not a single car was ever turned out for any customer during the Third Reich . . . By the time war started the Volkswagen factory turned to the manufacture of goods more useful to the army.

*The Rise and Fall of the Third Reich*,
William L. Shirer

*

'How many Jews can you get into a Volkswagen?' she asked.

'None,' I said. 'No Jew would get into a Volkswagen Beetle.'

I was lying. I had even owned a Volkswagen Beetle myself . . .

*Kalooki Nights*, Howard Jacobson

*

Volkswagen buyers are a special group. When you buy a Volkswagen, you don't just get a car; you also acquire a lot of friends

*Is Your Volkswagen a Sex Symbol?*,
Jean Risenbaum

\*

I was in a 1974 VW Beetle with torn seats and holes in the floorboard. The day was gray and bitter cold. The heater in my car didn't work . . . Sitting there in my VW Beetle, I knew two things: God loved me – desperately, achingly loved me – and all would be well.

*If Grace Is True: Why God Will Save Every Person*,
Philip Gulley, James Mulholland

\*

the peace comes from driving a
blue 67 Volks through the streets like a
teenager, radio tuned to The Host Who Loves You
Most, feeling the sun, feeling the solid hum
of the rebuilt motor
as you needle through traffic.

'One for the Shoeshine Man', Charles Bukowski

\*

At about four in the afternoon, Khomeini set out for Feiziyeh as planned . . . The crowds had gathered around Khomeini's residence as well as in the streets and courtyards of the shrine and the theological schools surrounding it. As it was impossible for Khomeini to move on foot, a pale green Volkswagen

'Beetle' convertible was brought to bear him through the crowd.

*Khomeini: Life of the Ayatollah*, Baqer Moin

*

Ali met the young fugitive at a café near Baghdad University. Saddam arrived in a Volkswagen Beetle and stepped out in a well-cut gray suit. These were exciting times for both men.

Mark Bowden, 'Tales of the Tyrant',
in *The New Kings of Non-Fiction*,
edited by Ira Glass

*

Serious themes are always presented with the hard edges smoothed over [on Iraqi TV]. In one episode of *Love and War*, Fawzi parks his Volkswagen Beetle, which then accidentally slips out of gear and rolls down a hill towards a police checkpoint – and is riddled with bullets for failing to stop. The humour is laced with the acid taste of reality: scores of Iraqis die every month for driving too close to US convoys or failing to brake for checkpoints.

Charles Clover, 'Carry on Filming',
in *Financial Times Magazine*, 19 March 2005

*

I am reminded of a light-skinned, blue-eyed, Afro-American-featured individual who could have been taken for anything from a sun-tinged Anglo-Saxon, an Egyptian or a mixed-breed American Indian to a strayed member of certain Jewish tribes. This young man appeared one sunny Sunday afternoon on New York's Riverside Drive near 151st Street, where he disrupted the visual peace of the promenading throng by racing up in a shiny new Volkswagen Beetle decked out with a gleaming Rolls Royce radiator . . .

'The Little Man at Chehaw Station', Ralph Ellison

\*

*Chavez Rides Red Volkswagen to Victory*

Hugo Chavez, in a closely observed election, won 61.35% of the vote to secure his presidential bid on December 3rd, 2006. His closest rival, economic and political conservative Manuel Rosales, came in with 33.38% of the vote . . . Hugo drove to the polls in his red Volkswagen bug dressed in his signature red shirt, black pants and white sneakers. 'He dresses like he is one of us,' said one of his supporters, reflecting the mood of the majority of the people in this increasingly red nation.

*http://fruitsofourlabour.blogspot.com*
Monday, 4 December 2006

\*

In his Ray-Bans and buffed-out yellow Volkswagen convertible, he was still able to patrol the boulevards of West Hollywood like a banty rooster, frequently accompanied by a German shepherd named Rue . . . 'He'd pull right up at a red light, smile at a bunch of girls and with one smile he had 'em,' recalled Harry Gittes. 'It not only worked; it never *not* worked.'

*Five Easy Decades: How Jack Nicholson Became the Biggest Movie Star in Modern Times*,
Dennis McDougal

Several weeks later Adam and Rose, their children, their children's children, and their children's children's children celebrated Labor Day with a big picnic by the lake. And everyone laughed so when little Tod got the Volkswagen stuck in the sand.

*The Last Volkswagen*, Charles A. Sennewald

\*

'I'll bet you guys aren't strong enough to pick up that Volkswagen,' said Owen Meany. But of course they were strong; they were not only strong enough to lift Dr Dolder's Beetle – they were strong enough to carry it out of town.

*A Prayer for Owen Meany*, John Irving

\*

The author makes a tacit deal with the reader. You hand them a backpack. You ask them to place certain things in it – to remember, to keep in mind – as they make their way up the hill . . . If you hand them a yellow Volkswagen and they have to haul this to the top of the mountain – to the end of the story – and they find that this Volkswagen has nothing whatsoever to do with your story, you're going to have a very irritated reader on your hands.

Frank Conroy, quoted in
*Tools of the Writer's Craft* by Sands Hall

\*

Von Axthelm felt in his bones there was little chance of opening fire in January. The flying bomb's production was sluggish. A few days before he had toured the Volkswagen factory where the bomb was to be mass produced: the works had complained that since early August flying-bomb engineers had specified no fewer that 150 modifications requiring 131 new parts in the weapon.

*The Mare's Nest*, David Irving

\*

He ushers you into the black Managerial Volkswagen, and before you know it, you're on the freeways. Near the interchange of the San Diego and the Santa Monica, Zhlubb points to a stretch of pavement: 'Here's where I got my first glimpse of one. Driving a VW, just like mine. I couldn't believe my eyes.'

*Gravity's Rainbow*, Thomas Pynchon

## 1

A screaming comes across the tarmac. It has happened before, often, many, many millions of times. It is the sound of an air-cooled, flat-four, horizontally opposed Volkswagen engine. It is the hammer of cylinders and exhaust gas, the whine and rattle of broad tolerances that expand and contract without the benefit of liquid coolant. It is not a pretty sound exactly, but it is ubiquitous (or was), a clattering across time and space, from 1930s' Germany to late-twentieth-century California to now, from factories in Wolfsburg, in Mexico and Brazil, from production lines in South Africa and Australia, in Thailand and Indonesia and Nigeria. Through deserts and swamps, across tundra and open water, it comes, solid, basic, reliable, mutable, capable of radical transformation while remaining itself, adept at absorbing punishment and meaning and grudging affection. The Love Bug. Yeah, right. World domination by any other name. The rest is rolling, moving, repeated history.

## 2

My name is Ian Blackwater and I'm a writer. I offer my apologies and I accept your commiserations. Some years ago I wrote a novel called *Volkswagens and Velociraptors*: you could describe it as a dystopian satire, I suppose, if that was the way you were inclined to describe things.

It was set in a devastated future when the vast majority of the world's population had been destroyed by some terminal though non-specific catastrophe. I told myself that the very vagueness of the catastrophe gave it a timeless, resonant, poetic quality. The only survivors of the disaster, it appeared at first, were the obsessive members of a London-based Volkswagen Beetle owners' club. They had been holding a club meeting in an underground car park when the Apocalypse struck. They were trapped in there for a good few days and that was what had allowed them to live.

Eventually these twenty or so Beetle owners and their cars emerged from the underground car park and drove out into a depopulated but largely undamaged London where they now had the complete run of the place. They got in their cars and screamed around an empty and unregulated London, doing doughnuts and handbrake turns outside the Houses of Parliament, drag racing along the Strand, pulling wheelies on the grass of Regent's Park, playing chicken on the Westway flyover. They were happy as clams. There was no law, no speed limits, no need for tax, insurance or brakes that worked. They had all the petrol they needed, and since they were the only twenty drivers in the world, environmental pollution suddenly didn't seem like much of a problem. They were free. Of course some of them were a bit choked up to have lost friends, families and other loved ones, but the majority of them thought this was a reasonable trade off for the automotive liberty they now enjoyed.

Things went well for a while but wouldn't you know it, unexpected and unforeseen trouble lay ahead. Deep in the tunnels of the London Tube system something was stirring. A group of prehistoric velociraptors that had been trapped in suspended animation in the bowels of the earth for millions of years suddenly, because of the catastrophe, found themselves re-animated, alive, awake and seriously pissed off. They emerged from the tunnels and the deserted Tube stations intent on killing everything they saw.

When I began writing the book, I knew a certain amount about Volkswagen Beetles, and very little indeed about velociraptors, and obviously to an extent I chose the latter for their alliterative potential as much as anything else. So I had to do my research. Velociraptors, I discovered, were a kind of dinosaur that lived seventy to eighty million years ago, fierce, bipedal, with a sickle-shaped claw on each foot, carni-vorous, growing up to seven feet long, and feathered. The name means swift thief, which I liked. And of course they made an appearance in the Stephen

Spielberg movie *Jurassic Park*, where they were shown larger than the reality, and they certainly weren't feathered: I guess Spielberg reckoned feathers weren't scary enough. But frankly when a seven-foot-long carnivorous, predatory dinosaur is coming at you, I don't think the feathers are going to be any source of comfort.

Substantial sections of my novel consisted of our heroes careening around London in their Beetles, trying desperately to escape from bands of marauding velociraptors, and occasionally mounting equally desperate, and largely useless, counter-attacks. This might have gone on for ever – certainly some of the book's reviewers said it went on far too long in my narrative – but eventually a leader emerged from among the Volkswagen folk.

The Beetle, as many people know, was the brain-child of Adolf Hitler. Before it was the People's Car it was the KdF-Wagen, KdF standing for Kraft durch Freude, 'strength through joy', which was the name of a Nazi-based health and leisure movement in pre-Second World War Germany. The car played a full part in the Nazi fantasy, not least because it could be, and in due course was, easily adapted to military use, and the factories that had made Volkswagen cars subsequently made flying bombs.

And so, in *Volkswagens and Velociraptors* the emerging hero, a man called Troy, gradually turns into a little Hitler. He plans, he marshals his troops, he gets them to wear cool uniforms, does some small-scale Nuremberg-style displays of strength, and after many an adventure he comes up with a way to destroy the velociraptors. He succeeds. The velociraptors lose

14

and are killed. However, when the battles are over Troy is still very much in control, talking about expanding his powers by way of a Reich that will last for a thousand years, and as it happens, the other Beetle owners are right behind him. The destruction of one race of monsters has created another.

There were a few sub plots, plenty of perverse sex, a love story and numerous digressions about the history of the Volkswagen Beetle, describing how it threw off its Nazi roots and became a genuine People's Car, known all over the world, loved by hippies, surfers, drag racers, Mexican taxi drivers, South American dictators, and so on.

Sales of the book were 'modest', but in some quarters it was regularly described as a 'cult novel', not that I can imagine any writer worth his salt being completely happy that his work was at the centre of a cult.

In the interviews I did to publicise the novel I spent a lot of time saying this wasn't really a science-fiction story, and that it wasn't even really a story about Volkswagens and velociraptors, any more than *Moby Dick* was really a story about an aquatic mammal. I said the Volkswagen Beetle was a symbol, and then interviewers would ask, 'What's it a symbol of?' And I'd say, 'Well, what do you have that needs symbolising?' And then I was accused of being a clever dick.

There was, from the beginning, a certain amount of 'movie interest' in the novel, which in my experience is far less exciting than you might imagine. What happens is that someone who calls himself or herself a producer comes along and gives you a surprisingly small amount of money, and this buys them the right to spend a year or so trying to 'develop' the project, raise some funds, pay to have a script written, perhaps get a well-known actor involved, and so on. When all this comes to nothing the rights go back to the author. As with prostitution, this isn't such a bad deal. You've got it, you sell it, you've still got it.

The movie rights to *Volkswagens and Velociraptors* were sold almost immediately, to a bright, enthusiastic young guy from the world of British TV comedy. We had lunch. Then a year passed, nothing much happened, and the rights came back. And so it went on for the next decade or so; various interested parties came and went – producers, directors, a couple of scriptwriters, even an animator – all of them telling me they had the vision and the connections to turn my work into a movie. I never believed any of them, though I'm sure they weren't exactly lying. They did no doubt have a vision, of sorts, and they surely did have some connections, but these were never powerful or grand enough to will the movie into being. For a little over ten years I regularly received small cheques and no movie got made.

And then incredibly, improbably, word started seeping through from my agent that the people who currently owned the movie rights, a company called Heat Exchanger and a director called Josh Martin, were making things happen. A script had been written; a script that a lot of people liked. I was asked if I wanted to read it and I said yes, but before a copy ever found its way to me, I heard that the funding for the production had been raised, casting had taken place, and for tax reasons the shooting had to start immediately. I was pleased and utterly amazed.

I know that authors are supposed to be terribly sensitive and fretful about what the crass and vulgar movie industry is going to do to their babies, but in this case I felt pretty sanguine about the whole business. A fair amount of time had passed since I'd written the book. I had been getting on with my life and writing other books, better books it seemed to me. *Volkswagens and Velociraptors* now felt like an 'early work', one that I liked well enough, but one I didn't feel especially protective towards.

Also, for what it was worth, I didn't actually see how they were going to make this movie. Even though the novel contained elements that were undoubtedly visual, indeed cinematic, it also presented some major problems. Computer graphics could certainly create velociraptors, but I knew that such things were very expensive, and that even the best of them can sometimes look very cheap. More than that, I couldn't imagine any way of creating a convincingly empty, post-Apocalyptic London. If the movie got the monsters and the empty city wrong it would surely be just laughable. There was also the more fundamental question of whether anybody really wanted to see a movie in which the central character drives a Volkswagen Beetle and turns into Adolf Hitler. Josh Martin and his backers evidently thought so.

I had never met Josh Martin, although we'd exchanged a couple of informal emails. In fact, until he bought the rights to *Volkswagens and Velociraptors* I'd never even heard of him, but I knew people who had, and they reckoned he was good news. I looked him up online and discovered he was youngish, at least for a movie director, he'd made a couple of quirky, Indie movies that had done well on the film-festival circuit, and that he'd directed a ton of music videos. He was also American, but I saw no problem with that. I didn't even see there was much of a problem when I heard that the movie was transferring the action from Britain to America, in fact to California. It seemed to me that an empty, post-Apocalyptic Los Angeles could be just as impressive as an empty, post-Apocalyptic London, and it would no doubt help with the international market.

The fact was, in the years since I'd written my book, the Volkswagen Beetle situation had changed a great deal. For one thing, there was now a car on the roads that called itself the New Beetle. It was based on the Volkswagen Golf, and it had nothing in common with the old Beetle, except a vague, willed physical resemblance, and we need never speak of it again.

Meanwhile the old Beetle had become much less common on the roads of England. Natural selection and obsolescence, whether planned or not, had killed off a great many of them. There were still English Beetle enthusiasts, there were owners' clubs and rallies and Bug-Jams, but the cars themselves were becoming rarer, turning into a special interest, into collectors' items. For cars that had been so numerous, so ordinary, so much a part of the landscape, this seemed all wrong. It made me feel old. And I knew that in California, where motor culture thrived, where the sun shone, where the winters weren't orgies of snow, ice and road salt, Beetles were still very much in business as daily drives as well as cult objects. Making the movie there made a lot of sense. I didn't fret. I felt very grown up about the whole business.

However, when I suddenly got an unexpected phone call from Josh Martin, the man himself, it was apparent that he thought I needed to be appeased. He sounded enthusiastic and confident, but also strangely cautious. He said he had written the script himself, and it was a great script. He had a great crew and a great cast. He had a great production designer who even as we spoke was making some fabulous working drawings for customised Beetles.

And then we got to the subject that he obviously felt uneasy and apologetic about. I asked him where exactly he was going to be shooting the film. He said, 'In a trailer park in Fontinella.'

I'd never heard of the place.

'It's a ways outside of LA,' Josh Martin said. 'Maybe seventy miles inland. I think Frank Zappa mentioned it in one his songs. It's kind of an industrial wasteland.'

'Industrial wasteland sounds OK,' I said.

'Yes, it is. It's more than OK.'

And then there was a pause, followed by what sounded like a prepared speech.

'Look, Ian,' he said, 'I admit that budgetary considerations came into our choice of location, but you know, they always do. And often it's no bad thing. And the fact is, there were creative reasons too. A whole city is a vast, borderless canvas, and that can create a lack of focus. By concentrating the action in a closed community, like a trailer park, everything becomes more intense, more focused and filmic.'

I didn't argue with him. How could I have, and what would have been the point? It was his decision to make, not mine. He might have even been right for all I knew, and in truth I was flattered that he thought he had to concern himself with my feelings at all.

'Seriously,' he said, 'I think you're going to be really pleased by what I've done with your novel, and what I'm going to do. And that's really, really important to me.'

I should probably have started fretting right then.

'Anyway,' he said, 'you'll see when you get here. There's a plane ticket on its way to you.'

Ah yes, the plane ticket. There was a clause in the contract, negotiated by my agent on one of her better days, saying that I was entitled to visit the set at the film company's expense. I was to be given accommodation, shown respect and a good time. This had always sounded like the best part of the whole deal, though the most unlikely one.

I was living in rural Suffolk at the time, trying to make my writer's income stretch that bit further, and when I'd thought the movie was going to be filmed in London I'd imagined being housed at some fine, swanky Park Lane hotel with fawning staff and limitless room service. OK, so that wasn't to be. No sweat. A trip to America was, in all sorts of ways, a much better perk: but quite what sort of swanky hotels they had in the industrial wasteland of Fontinella remained to be seen, and I was all too eager to see.

## 3

I did my research on Fontinella. It was, as Josh Martin had already told me, a good way inland from Los Angeles, perhaps an hour and a half's drive, though close to the Interstate. On the town website it claimed to have an old main street that was a piece of classic Americana, though there were no photographs to prove it. It also had big railway yards, various industries that served the trucking and scrap-metal industries, and a lot of trailer parks. As far as I could tell, not many movies had been shot there.

My plane ticket came. Its date was a little way in the future. They would be a couple of weeks into shooting by the time I got there. That was OK by me, and it really made no difference. I would have nothing to do on the shoot. I knew I wouldn't be a real part of the team. I'd simply drift around, be nice to everybody, have them be nice back, and then I'd leave a week later.

People who knew about these things told me that a week was a long time to hang around a movie shoot with nothing to do. In fact they told me that life on a movie shoot was boring at the best of times, and sometimes it could drive you absolutely insane. I didn't doubt that, but like most writers I reckoned I didn't bore easily and I'd always been very good at finding things to amuse myself. I thought I'd be able to cope. In any case, weren't movie shoots supposed to be arenas of debauchery and bad behaviour? No doubt that would relieve some of the boredom.

There had been talk of my girlfriend Caroline coming with me to Fontinella but in the end she decided to stay home. It didn't sound like much of a holiday, she said, and I agreed. She told me to bring back something nice for her from Rodeo Drive. I said I would, though I didn't know quite where Rodeo Drive was, or how I'd get there. I also said I'd call her often and promised I wouldn't 'get up to anything', all the time hoping there'd be opportunities to break that promise.

The ticket was for economy class, which was something of a disappointment, and the flight wasn't for Los Angeles, but for Ontario, not the Canadian one, but a place in California that was apparently convenient for Fontinella. That was the only thing about the flight that was convenient. It involved three separate planes and two awkward changes, one in Charlottesville, and one in Phoenix; a route that only made sense as a way of bringing down the ticket price. The movie was evidently on a tight budget, but that didn't come as a surprise.

I survived the flights, but it was nearly two in the morning before I'd picked up my luggage and stepped out into the arrivals area of Ontario International Airport, a space both homey and futuristic, where a small, delicately wiry, big-eyed young woman was holding up a sheet of cardboard with my name on it. She was ebony-skinned, black, African-American, of colour – or whatever the acceptable term is.

'Hi, Mr Blackwater. Welcome to America,' she said.

'Call me Ian,' I answered.

She smiled uncertainly, called me Ian, and told me her name was Cadence. 'You know, just the usual spelling,' she said, and then she quickly added, 'Wow, meeting the writer. This is so cool.'

'Only the writer of the book,' I said. 'I'm sure the writer of the screenplay is much cooler.'

'Oh no, books are way cooler.'

She seemed like someone I could do business with.

'So are you excited?' she asked.

'Well, I have some trepidation if that's what you mean. Or I would do if I weren't too tired to think.'

She offered to carry my bag and I was enough of a gentleman to decline. She led the way through the airport, out to the parking lot.

'Good flight?' she asked hesitantly. It sounded as though she knew that was the kind of thing you were supposed to ask people when they'd just got off a plane, but it didn't come naturally to her.

'Not really,' I said.

'I don't suppose you fly too much,' she said.

'Enough to know a good flight from a bad one.'

'So this is your first time in America?'

'No,' I said. I'd been there half a dozen times before, one way and another.

'But your first time here on the West Coast.'

'Actually not,' I said.

She sounded disappointed. I felt I was letting her down with my cosmopolitanism.

'But it's my first time flying to Ontario International, to go to Fontinella, in order to be on the set to see one of my novels turned into a movie.'

'Good,' she said, 'that's very good.'

I got the feeling that she wanted me to be some tweedy old professor who seldom left his book-lined study, much less his country. She seemed to think that having my own hair, teeth and limbs might be an indication that I wasn't quite a serious enough writer. Whether a tweedy, serious old professor was likely to have written a book like *Volkswagens and Velociraptors* was another matter.

We approached our ride, her car, a battered old Toyota. I hadn't really been expecting a limo, much less a Volkswagen Beetle, but I had been expecting something with fewer scrapes and dents, something on which the doors opened and closed without the major negotiations we now had to go through before we could get inside.

'Sorry it's not more glamorous,' Cadence said. 'And I guess it ought to be a hybrid to be politically correct. But it's mine and it's paid for.'

'I thought the film company would have given you a car,' I said.

'Yeah, you'd think that, wouldn't you?' she agreed.

She started to drive, purposefully but not very fast, out through the convolutions of the airport roads. I was so tired I was seeing things, flashes and dark shapes at the edges of my vision, but it seemed only polite to keep talking.

'How are things on the shoot?' I said.

'Well, I can't really say.'

'Is it a secret?'

'No, I mean I never worked on a movie before. I'm just an intern. I'm a nobody. They don't let me do much. Just shit work.'

'Like picking up the author at the airport.'

'Sorry.'

'It's OK.'

'So I don't have much to compare it to.'

I knew her reticence was saying something, though I couldn't tell what, and then she couldn't resist adding, 'Things seem a little tense. But maybe it's a creative tension.'

'I'll bet that's it,' I said, too out of it to know if I was being sarcastic or not.

We were free of the airport now and we drove for fifteen minutes or so, and then we stopped somewhere, although frankly it looked very much like nowhere. We were at a trailer park. A sign on the gate said 'Idle Palms' and it was true, there were a couple of gangly palm trees growing inside the entrance, and they weren't doing much. They were a bit ratty and careworn, but to a man who's just arrived in California from England they still seemed perfectly exotic.

In fact the trailer park itself was a little oasis of greenery and humanity, neat, clean and well ordered. Individual trailers were lined up in geometrically precise rows. Some had carports and canopies, and potted plants by the front door and ornate fake street-lamps.

Outside the walls of the park however was a chaos of concrete and metal. On one side was a raised freeway that hummed and growled with traffic even at that time of night, and beneath it was a scrapyard stacked high with dead cars. On the other side was a small stadium, a sort of motor-racing circuit that called itself the Fontinella Speedway, visible but impenetrable behind receding planes of barbed wire and chain-link fencing.

We drove in through the gateway of the trailer park and immediately I saw a row of Volkswagen Beetles lined up inside. They'd been gleefully hacked about and customised. Various crucial parts had been amputated and replaced with exotic prosthetics – wings, fins, spoilers, spikes, battering rams – then the cars had been painted in gloriously clashing colours and decorated with cool though unfamiliar symbols and logos, some of them just a little like swastikas. I was enough of a petrol head and a Beetle freak that the sight did my heart good. It made the movie seem infinitely more real.

'These are for the movie, right?' I said, and I realised that was a silly thing to say. What else would they be for?

'Sure, it's all for the movie,' Cadence said. 'That place over there is where the velociraptors breed. Over there's where the Volkswagen warriors live.'

'So? What?' I said. 'This is the movie set?'

I was confused. It was nice enough of her to have brought me here, to see where the movie was being shot, but I thought it could surely have waited till the morning. Right then I had much greater need of a room and a bed.

'Sure,' Cadence said. 'It's the set. It's also the production office. And it's where we all live. Most of us, anyway. Not Josh Martin.'

'Where does he live?'

'God knows. His own private Kosovo maybe.'

'Huh?'

'He has a place in the Hollywood Hills. He commutes every day in his Porsche Carrera.'

'Well, a Porsche is a half-brother to a Beetle,' I said.

She looked at me blankly.

'Ferdinand Porsche,' I said. 'He designed the Beetle as well as the Porsche.'

Her blankness remained intact. I felt like an idiot.

'Right. That's your place over there,' she said.

She pointed at a trailer pressed up against the fence that separated the trailer park from the speedway next door. The trailer was small but quite cool looking; maybe not as cool or as elegant as a genuine, blob-like, aluminium Airstream, but it was trying hard. Of course I'd heard that Hollywood stars are provided with trailers, some of them vast, luxurious things apparently, but I didn't think they actually lived in them.

'Yours is one of the better ones,' Cadence said. 'And you've got it to yourself. I'm sharing mine with five other people.'

Was that supposed to make me feel bad or good? It was nice that I was being treated well, but when the VIP treatment consisted of a trailer pressed up against a chain-link fence I had to wonder just how high the production values were.

'Yeah,' said Cadence, doing a fair job of mind reading. 'All the money's going to be up on the screen. I believe that's what we're supposed to say.'

# 4

# The Pope's Revisions

I don't suppose the Pope, any Pope, does a great deal of driving. Possibly some Popes have been motoring enthusiasts in their earlier life, but once they become Supreme Pontiff the opportunities for putting the pedal to the metal must surely be severely limited.

I think we can safely say that Pope John Paul II, né Karol Wojtyla, was no great fan of German automobile technology. Not least of the indignities he had to endure under the Nazi occupation of his native Poland was being run down and seriously injured by a German truck in 1944 in the town of Wodawici. It's thought the accident may well have had some bearing on his decision to become a priest. He was ordained in 1946, and became Pope thirty-two years later in 1978.

That was the same year that Volkswagen stopped producing the Beetle in its European factories, though production continued in Latin America – in Brazil and especially in Mexico – right through into the next millennium; just.

Pope John Paul II visited Mexico five times, in 1979, 1990, 1997, 1999 and 2002. The last three trips were made after he'd already been diagnosed as suffering from Parkinson's disease, but that didn't get in the way of an enormous mutual affection between John Paul and the Mexican People. He even developed a catch phrase '*México – Siempre Fiel*' (Mexico, Ever Faithful).

In 2004, a large delegation of autoworkers from the Mexican Volkswagen plant in Puebla decided to show their own affection, and specifically their gratitude for the Pope's canonisation of Juan Diego in 2002. At a General Audience at the Vatican, this delegation presented the Pope with an 'Aquarius blue' Volkswagen Beetle. It was no ordinary Beetle. It was one of a limited edition, named the Ultima Edicion, the last three thousand genuine Beetles ever to be made anywhere in the world. It had actually been produced the previous year: Beetle production officially ended worldwide on 30 July 2003.

The Ultima Edicion had a higher spec than most Beetles: 1600cc engine, electronic fuel injection, halogen headlights, front disc brakes, factory-installed immobiliser. By some accounts (though not all) the car presented to the Pope was the very last Beetle ever made, which would make in number 21,529,464: other accounts place that particular car in the Volkswagen museum in Wolfsburg, which strikes me as far more likely. Either way, what better gift for an eighty-four-year-old man, by then suffering from a plethora of other illnesses in addition to Parkinson's disease, than a car he could never possibly drive? He was good enough to bless it anyway.

## 5

I woke up early in unfamiliar, and as I now saw, rather grubby surroundings. A lot of people had evidently slept in that trailer before me, and many had left their traces in the form of cigarette burns, gouges on the walls and ceilings, and anonymous stains everywhere else. Still I wasn't going to complain. If money was tight on the movie, who was I to expect special treatment?

I looked out through the trailer's scratched plastic window and saw a lot of people milling around, the film crew no doubt. They were an unlikely mix of surly, stocky, older white men and bright, lean, hip, multi-ethnic younger people of both sexes. It was hard to imagine how they all got along together, but at that moment they were unified in scooping up the breakfast buffet that was laid out on some trestle tables. I decided to join them.

My focus and concentration wasn't all it might have been, and it took me for ever to get washed and dressed. But at last, as I was ready and about to go outside and face this strange new world, there was a pounding on the trailer door, which then flew open despite being locked. And there stood Josh Martin, my director. He looked older, fatter, wearier, than in his online picture, but then I suppose we all do. He looked more suntanned too. I said hello: he didn't.

'These people,' he snarled. 'These fucking people.'
And he made a grand gesture that seemed to take
in the whole world, me included.

'Which people?' I asked.

He looked at me as though only a complete
idiot wouldn't know exactly what he was talking
about, and at that moment, right on cue, I became
aware of a terrible clanking and hammering. It
was coming from near by, though not from inside
the trailer park, rather from the speedway next
door.

'Take a look at this shit,' he said, and we left the
trailer so he could show me what was going on.

In the hot light of morning I could see just how close
together the trailer park and the speedway were. Last
night the stadium had looked deserted, but now there
were many signs of intense though unfathomable
activity, people running around carrying power
tools and large pieces of plywood. Engines were
being revved, sheet metal was being hammered, glass
was being pulverised. It all seemed, in fact, very much
the sort of noise and activity that might be expected
to come from something that called itself a speedway.
For that matter, I now saw there were a few Volkswagen Beetles on the other side of the fence, inside
the speedway grounds. These weren't customised or
exotically painted like the ones connected with the
movie, in fact most of them looked like non-runners,
but it suggested to me that the speedway folk might
be natural allies rather than the 'fucking people'
Josh Martin said they were. Of course I knew nothing about it.

At that moment the air was split by the metal

31

seething of a frighteningly powerful electric saw. I jumped several feet.

'That must be hard to live with,' I said.

'Oh you think?' Josh Martin said. 'And what if you were trying to make a fucking movie? What if you were trying to record some fucking live fucking sound?'

'I can see your problem,' I said.

'You can't see the half of it,' he said.

I didn't doubt that he was right but I couldn't see what I was supposed to do other than offer abject sympathy. For a moment he became slightly quieter and more thoughtful, more sorry for himself possibly.

'I was told it was abandoned,' he said. 'The old abandoned Fontinella Speedway. That's what everybody always calls it. But now there's a fucking freak show going on in there.'

He had a point. Now that I'd had a better look, I could see that the people working on the other side of the fence were a wild bunch, all bare chests and shaved heads, tattoos and piercings and overcomplicated facial hair. And by no means all of them were men.

Mostly they were doing things with cars, but they certainly weren't doing anything as straightforward as repairing them or making them run. Some people were erecting scaffolding towers, building a stage, constructing a couple of ramps. It was too early to make a judgement, but my immediate impression was that everybody on the speedway side of the fence was working much more purposefully and enthusiastically that anybody on the movie set.

'Does the noise ever stop?' I asked.

32

'Oh sure,' said Josh Martin. 'When we're shooting, then they stop.'

That sounded like a good thing. 'Good,' I said.

'Well, let me qualify that,' he said. 'What actually happens is that before I say, "Action," somebody has to go over there with a bagful of cash, and hand it over and that buys us about five minutes of quiet from those bastards. They've got me by the prostate.'

I could see it wasn't a perfect arrangement.

'And it's making a big fucking hole in the budget,' Josh Martin said angrily. 'Still, the author's here now, everything's going to be just fucking peachy.'

With that he wandered over to the table where the breakfast buffet had been laid out. He looked at it briefly with disgust and then fell into intense conversation with one of the stocky white men and together they went off, to do something filmic, I assumed, something that had nothing to do with me. I went over to look at the remains of the breakfast and I understood Josh Martin's disgust. The buffet had been reduced to a few mangled and half-chewed remnants.

'Yeah, you got to get up early in the morning to beat the Teamsters,' said a young female voice behind me.

'Not that the breakfast's worth getting up early for anyway,' said another voice, a man's.

I turned and saw two people standing there. They were, there could be no doubt about it, a couple of actors. More than that, given the outfits they were wearing – tattered futuristic jump suits decked out with Volkswagen insignia – they were obviously dressed as characters from my book, from the movie.

33

The actress was a tall blonde, quirkily good-looking, managing to be simultaneously willowy and muscular. The actor was a dwarf.

'So,' said the woman, 'am I the way you pictured Natasha?'

Natasha was the nearest thing my book had to a heroine, or perhaps anti-heroine. She was in love with Troy: the Eva Braun of the story. This flesh-and-blood Natasha looked like a perfectly good piece of casting, but the truth was I didn't have a very specific idea of how she, or any of my characters, was supposed to look. Maybe some authors have a solid visual image of their creations, but I never do, and especially not of their faces. Sure they have qualities: they're old or young, fat or thin, good or bad, sexually attractive or not, but that's about as much detail as I like to give. Partly it's so that readers can use their imagination to create their own pictures, but it's also so as not to alienate the less imaginative. If I say a character has red hair, hazel eyes and small breasts, well some people are going to really love those things and think I'm describing a really great-looking woman, but others will hate red hair, hazel eyes and small breasts and therefore not think that the character's good looking at all. So I tend to use more general or abstract descriptions: she was simultaneously willowy and muscular; and sometimes I just describe someone as 'attractive', and let the reader fill in the blanks according to taste.

I didn't want to get into all that with an actress I was meeting for the first time, so I said, without giving it a great deal of thought, 'You're much sexier than I imagined,' and I felt like a complete idiot the moment it was out of my mouth.

She gave me a complex, ambiguous look and maybe a quarter of a smile. She was evidently flattered but she was also suspicious. Was I just being an arse licker and creep, or was I perhaps being a snide, sarcastic Englishman and implying that she was glossy and vacuous and wrong for the part? I wasn't doing that, but how could I have convinced her on such limited acquaintance?

'Really,' I said. 'You're much better for the part than I could ever have imagined.'

'I can see I'm going to have to watch you,' she said.

I wasn't unhappy for her to watch me.

'And what about me?' said the dwarf.

Well, it's a funny thing isn't it, I thought to myself. Once upon a time a writer sat in his room back in England, some good while ago, writing a book, and he realised he'd given himself a lot of problems, chiefly that he had too many characters, all of them Volkswagen enthusiasts, and he was having trouble differentiating one from another. Then he thought of a really crass, obvious way of distinguishing one of them: he made him a dwarf. It wasn't a very original idea, and it took the writer all of three seconds to set down the line, 'Ronnie was a dwarf,' yet here and now, a decade or so later, five and a half thousand miles away from home, this thought had been made flesh.

I looked at the actor playing the part of this dwarf character that I'd so casually and so thoughtlessly created, and I didn't know what to say.

'Don't tell me,' he said; 'you pictured someone shorter.'

I thought he was trying to be funny, so I laughed,

though not too hard, in case he *wasn't*. Fortunately the dwarf found his own remark just about the funniest thing he'd ever heard, and he slapped me hard on the lower back.

'You'll get along just fine around here, Ian,' he said, and I did hope he knew what he was talking about.

## 6

I gathered together a few feeble breakfast remnants, picked at them, and waited for something to happen. I suppose it did eventually, though I soon saw I might have to redefine my notions of 'something' and 'happen'. A lot of slothful, half-hearted activity eventually coalesced around one of the trailers. A scene was being shot that I could just about recognise as having something to do with my book. It was based on an episode from early in the narrative when two of the Volkswagen survivors first discover what turn out to be velociraptor eggs. In the novel the discovery is made in the ticket office of a wrecked London Underground station. But here the eggs were to be found clinging to the underside of a Baja Beetle: a particularly fine, rugged, bright yellow example of the breed was being used.

The 'action', and there's an interesting word, now consisted of Natasha and Ronnie the dwarf lying on the ground shining torches up under the Baja's chassis, saying very little but doing a whole lot of reacting. At least that's what I was led to believe. Actors, crew, camera, lights, sound boom, were all arrayed at ground level, and what with all the reflectors and tripods and ancillary people standing around, I couldn't see a thing.

Certainly to the untrained eye, such as mine, it

seemed that nothing was going on, but then I had only the vaguest idea of what was *supposed* to be going on. Movies, I knew, were created by a slow, painstaking process. Perhaps everything was going absolutely to plan. True, Josh Martin looked stressed and manic, but from what little I'd seen, that might well have been his default mode. Everybody else looked untroubled, or at least indifferent.

Hours went by, and I realised that nobody had lied about the essential dullness of hanging around a movie set with nothing to do. In fact even those people who did have something to do seemed to be finding it pretty dull too. But I did get my first glimpse of how the movie bought its silence. At rare and widely spaced intervals they were eventually ready to do a take, at which time there was much mumbling into walkie-talkies, and then someone, usually Cadence, my greeter from the previous night, hopped on a bicycle, carrying a small bag of money, and pedalled off to the speedway next door. Shortly thereafter all the noise stopped, there was a shout of, 'Action,' the cameras rolled for perhaps thirty seconds, the actors acted, then there was a shout of, 'Cut,' perhaps followed by, 'Let's do it again,' or, 'Check the gate,' and when they were finished, at most a couple of minutes later, there'd be more use of the walkie-talkies and then the noise from next door would start up again. It seemed a mad, laborious and ramshackle system, but evidently a workable one.

Events continued to unfold slowly, and most of them barely counted as events at all. Actors and crew moved from one area of the trailer park to another.

Shots were set up, silence fell, performances were given, then it was over for a while, and then the process repeated itself again, and again. It wasn't glamorous and it wasn't any fun to watch, but why should it have been? It was an industrial process, like making pig iron.

I amused myself briefly by looking at some of the Beetles that had been created for the film. They now looked a lot less impressive than they had last night. I could see that the spoilers, fins and so on were flimsy constructions, made of cardboard and papier mâché, and glued clumsily to the underlying car bodies. The essential blotchy, ham-fistedness of the painting was now visible too. Still, I told myself, it might all come over very different on film. I also looked around hoping I might see the models or animatronics or robots or puppets or whatever they were using to replicate the velociraptors, but there was no sign of them anywhere.

I was treated well enough by the people I encountered. At the beginning of the day, naturally enough, they didn't know who I was. I could have been an accountant or a union official, and they viewed me with the appropriate suspicion. But gradually word got out that I was 'the author' and everyone treated me far more sympathetically, although sometimes they displayed the sort of chilly kindness you might extend to a sickly old man you knew wasn't long for this world. I smiled a lot, and exchanged the occasional word, but I certainly didn't have anything that counted as a conversation.

Eventually the long day came to an end. The shooting was declared to be over and we had dinner.

It was a surprisingly humble affair. Weren't directors supposed to cook huge spaghetti dinners for the whole cast and crew, and thereby create an aura of festive and artistic *bonhomie*? Not here. A number of picnic tables had been set up in one of the slightly pleasanter corners of the trailer park, but these things are only comparative. Worse than that, there appeared to be a fierce hierarchical structure at work. The bright, lean, hip, young, multi-ethnic crew members crowded together at one of the tables, while the surly, stocky, older white men sat at another. Meanwhile the 'talent', which included the actors, Josh Martin and what looked like an inner circle of his cronies – cinematographer, assistant director *et al.* – were at another. Each table tried hard to avoid all contact with the others.

I didn't feel I belonged in any of these groups but I sat with the 'talent', between the two actors playing Natasha and Ronnie: I had no idea what their actual names were. Nobody was very chatty, certainly not with me, but not much with each other either. They did talk just a little bit about work, about acting and film-making, but not about the work they were actually doing here. They talked about other jobs they'd had, about jobs they hoped to get in the future, about the times they'd worked with David Carradine or Sally Kellerman, but they didn't say a word about the film they were actually making.

Given how slowly things had happened during the day I was amazed at how quickly everybody ate and left the tables. It was like a school canteen. There was nothing for me to do but go back to my trailer. I was tired: the jet lag, the strange surroundings, the endless smiling at people I didn't know. I thought about calling my girlfriend back in England, and realised I should have done it much earlier. In England it was now the middle of the night. She wouldn't want to hear from me *that* much.

There was a TV in my trailer. It only got half a dozen stations but they were all strange and foreign enough to keep me entertained, or they would have been in other circumstances. As soon as I started watching I dozed off, and then kept waking up with a start, not knowing where I was. I also kept hearing, or thought I did, loud, violent, not quite identifiable sounds, though I couldn't be sure whether they were coming from the TV, the outside world or my dreams.

And then there was a knock on my door. It was gentle, considerate, definitely not a Josh Martin production. I opened up and there stood Cadence.

'How you doing?' she asked.

'Fine,' I said.

'Jet lag?'

'Sure.'

'Bored?'

'Oh yeah,' I said.

'Thought you might be. Here.'

She was carrying a couple of bottles of Mexican beer. She handed me one and kept one for herself.

'I guess you have beer in England. But this is a little bit of Americana,'

'Mexicana?' I said, looking at the label on the bottle.

'Same difference.'

I wasn't really in much shape to make cheerful conversation, and Cadence seemed less than a great conversationalist; still I wanted to be friendly, and

41

on my first full day in Fontinella it seemed rather more civilised to be talking to somebody than to be sitting alone and falling asleep watching TV.

'Come in, sit down,' I said.

She did and looked around with a mixture of envy and resentment.

'This is really comparatively luxurious,' she said. 'So, do you want to talk about literature?'

'Er, maybe another time,' I said.

'OK. Want to talk about Volkswagens?'

'Why not?'

'I'd never even been in one till I started working on this movie.'

'No?'

'No. It's not really a car the brothers drive.'

'That's true in England too.'

And then she asked me a terrible question: 'So what kind of Beetle do you drive?'

The fact was I'd owned and driven a lot of Volkswagens in my time, a number of Beetles, a camper and one very smart Karmann Ghia. Some had been good, a couple had been lemons, but on balance I was still very Beetle positive. However, what I liked best about Beetles was their past, their back-story, and the fact that they brought with them a trailer full of cultural and historical baggage. I wasn't a full-blown Beetle obsessive myself, not really, not compared to some of the obsessives I'd met, but I completely saw how you could be. Above all, I thought, Beetles were great fun to write about; rather more fun than to own or drive. And as I said, *Volkswagens and Velociraptors* had been written a while back. I had moved on, not very far, and certainly not any great distance

42

upwards, but the sad truth was that these days I drove a Ford Focus.

I tried my best to explain this to Cadence, but she didn't like it. She really didn't. I was disappointing her all over again. Back in England, not driving a Beetle had never seemed like a cause for shame, but here and now, in California on this movie set, it seemed to demonstrate that I was a complete fake and trifler.

Cadence finished her beer and said, 'I'd better be getting back.'

'Must you?' I asked.

She shrugged. If I wasn't a real Beetle enthusiast then it seemed I wasn't entitled to her company. I went to bed but I slept no better than I had earlier. I heard the same sounds as before, though now they seemed much stranger. Some of them were definitely human voices: it could have been the sound of partying, of people whooping it up and having a good time, but it could just as easily have been the sound of angry people arguing and shouting at each other. And sometimes it didn't sound human at all, as if it might have been dogs or wolves, or for all I knew, velociraptors.

# 7

# The Cannibal Beetle

Joachim Kroll was known as the Cannibal Killer, but not always, obviously. It took the German police over twenty years to work out that he was either of these things. For most of his life he was known around his hometown of Duisberg as a likeable man with an IQ of 76 who kept a collection of dolls in his apartment and invited little girls from the neighbourhood in to play with them. What could be more innocent? He had other dolls in his apartment too, full-size female sex dolls on which, among other activities, he practised his strangulation technique.

Between 1955 and 1976, according to his own confession, he raped and murdered at least fourteen females. There may well have been others: he admitted that his memory was vague on some of the details. At least two of the victims were under five.

Kroll's motives for the killings were primarily sexual, and in general he had no interest in murdering men. However, on 22 August 1965, by the lake in Grossenbaum, a few miles south of Duisberg, Kroll encountered the unfortunate Herman Schmitz who was with his girlfriend, generally known as 'Rita' in the literature, though that is not her real name. The couple was having sex in the front seat of Schmitz's

Volkswagen Beetle, unaware that Joachim Kroll was standing hidden outside, looking in through the window of the car and spying on them.

After a while Kroll's voyeurism caused him to become uncontrollably aroused and he felt the urgent need to rape and murder 'Rita'. He seems to have been concerned with Schmitz only in so far as he wanted to get him out of the way. And so, improbably and impractically, Kroll crawled along the ground, unseen, and jammed a knife into the Beetle's front tyre, which exploded with a loud bang.

Kroll had presumably expected Schmitz to get out of the car to investigate, but instead of doing that Schmitz started the engine and began to drive away. He didn't know the area, however, and drove in the wrong direction, into a dead end, giving Kroll time to catch up.

Schmitz turned the Beetle around in the dead end and was heading back the way he'd come when Kroll leapt in front of the car, waving his arms, begging Schmitz to stop. Even more improbably Schmitz now decided that Kroll was a harmless passer-by in need of help. He stopped the car and got out to talk to Kroll and offer assistance, leaving 'Rita' inside the car, from where she was able to watch as Kroll now stabbed her boyfriend in the stomach with his knife. Schmitz collapsed in agony.

'Rita' seems to have been rather smarter than her boyfriend: she got behind the wheel of the Beetle, set it in motion and tried to run Kroll down. She failed, and Kroll escaped through the woods. Herman Schmitz died of his injuries a few days later. He was Kroll's only male victim. The police saw no connection

45

between Schmitz's death and those of the women who had been raped and murdered in the area. Kroll would be able to enjoy another twelve years of murderous liberty.

## 8

The next day in Fontinella started much as the previous one had, and it threatened to go on in precisely that same dull way. I couldn't face it and so I decided to go for a walk. There weren't, in the ordinary sense, many places near by to go walking. The agglomeration of freeway, junk yard and now no longer abandoned speedway didn't look like obvious walking territory, but the fact is I've always been attracted to disuse and decay, to industrial ruin; and I actually found it intriguing.

I left the trailer park. There was a security guard on the gate, and his uniform made him look a lot like a cop, but a closer inspection of the shield-shaped badges on his arms, revealed that he worked for Celluloid Security, a name that I thought rather blew his credibility and authority. I nodded to him on the way out and he moved his head just enough to suggest that he might possibly be nodding back.

I began my walk, and found that the distances involved were much longer than I'd imagined. The trailer park itself covered a surprisingly large area, and the grounds of the speedway, mostly consisting of parking lot, were huge. Walking once around the perimeter of the two would take up a lot of time, and that was good: I wanted my time taken up.

Even though the speedway was now occupied, it

47

still had an overall look of careworn neglect. There were great potholes in the entry road, and the few portable office buildings were falling apart. The only thing in good shape was the fence, enough to keep out any but the most determined trespassers. It wasn't obvious why the people inside needed so much protection, and it still wasn't even clear to me what they were actually doing in there, but as I walked past a side-entrance gate, I got a few clues.

I'd thought Josh Martin had been speaking metaphorically when he called the people next door a freak show, but in fact they were, or at least claimed to be, the real thing. There was a sign attached to the gate that said, 'Motorhead Phil's Famous Automotive Freak Show'. That in itself begged as many questions as it answered, but it came with an illustration, a painted fairground sign that made things just a little clearer. It was a garish illustration of an airborne car, flying over a gorge of terrifying depth. The vehicle was on fire and a tail of devilish flames trailed behind it. It was a rather generic illustration of a car, but it could very well have been a Volkswagen Beetle, and perhaps it would have been if the painter had been more skilled.

I was surprised to find the gate unlocked and open just a little, and although it wasn't exactly welcoming, it allowed me to see a few Beetles lined up inside. And again it struck me as odd that there was such apparent antagonism between the movie folk and the speedway people. Surely a shared taste for Volkswagen Beetles ought to be enough to enable them to get along, at least temporarily. It even occurred to me, though I knew it was totally none of my business, that it might be a help if Josh Martin invited some of the freak show crew to be involved with the movie, maybe as extras: they were certainly an eye-catching bunch.

I peered at the row of Beetles inside the gate, and I could see they were mostly wrecks, but one of them at least was in interestingly distressed condition. In the way that I enjoy industrial ruin, I also like things that have some patina to them: houses, furniture, music, people. And especially cars. This Beetle fitted the bill nicely.

It looked as though it must once have been something very nice indeed – Cal-look, unostentatiously customised; lowered, dechromed, bumpers and running boards removed. The paintwork had apparently started out as a thick, melting shade of pale sky blue, and then a hot sun had burned it paler still. After that, if I'd had to guess, I'd have said the car had spent some time at the coast where it had been splattered by giant waves of salt water that had given it an overall rash of rusty pockmarks. Add to that all the scrapes and scratches, prangs and dings and dents that bodywork is heir to, and you were left with the thing at which I was now looking, a uniquely and elegantly beat up Volkswagen Beetle. I thought it was magnificent.

I slipped inside the gate to have a closer look, and then I saw there was a man sitting behind the wheel of the car, a fat man, a very fat man indeed. I stopped in my tracks: I didn't want to look like a trespasser. But he saw me and waved and beckoned to me in an all too demanding way. Reluctantly I went over to him.

'How's it going?' I asked breezily.

'Not so good,' he said. 'My car won't start. And I'm really depressed.'

I had some sympathy. A car that won't start can cast a pall of gloom over the most inherently optimistic of us, and the fat man in the car didn't look inherently optimistic.

'Can you help me out? Give me a push?' he asked.

He had a curious accent. I thought it sounded vaguely English, but I knew I could be wrong about that.

'All right,' I said. I could see no reason not to be helpful. Plenty of people had helped me out in the days when I'd owned an unreliable Beetle, and I was happy enough to return the favour. A good push and a bump start was often all that was needed to kick a Beetle into life.

I took up position at the rear of the car and waited for the driver to get out so we could push together. I stood there for a while and nothing happened. I looked at the guy, but he looked at the road ahead and stayed right where he was.

'Aren't you going to get out?' I called.

'No,' he said flatly, and then added. 'I can't.'

I thought a bit more explanation was required but none was forthcoming. We could have stayed like that for ever.

'What do you mean?' I asked.

'I can't get out of the car,' he said, 'I'm too fat. It's really depressing.'

I looked at him more closely, and yes, he was a whale of a man, shapeless and blubbery and apparently far wider than the door of a Volkswagen Beetle.

'How did you get in there?' I said.

'I wasn't this fat when I got in,' he replied.

I couldn't tell if he was joking or not, but I didn't want to drag this out any longer than necessary. I summoned up such strength as I had and I started to push the Beetle with the guy inside. The car moved, but not very far and not very fast, and it certainly didn't pick up enough speed to make a bump start possible. After a prolonged bout of pushing we had barely got through the speedway gate to the road outside. The road was straight and flat without the kind of easy downward slope that would have encouraged the car to start. I looked around to see if there was anybody to hand who might join in with the pushing but the whole area was utterly deserted.

'If you could just push me over there, that would be great,' the fat man said.

He pointed down the road in the direction of a long, low building made of pink-painted cinder blocks that I could just make out as a diner. It was tucked in under a concrete ramp, and it had a sign outside that told me I was looking at an establishment called El Puerco Loco, the Crazy Pig if I remembered my Spanish. It was adorned with a large plastic figure of a cheerfully demented cartoon porker. It was perhaps two hundred and fifty yards away, a fair distance when you're pushing a Volkswagen Beetle and its occupant, but I felt I had no choice.

'I haven't eaten for ages,' the man said.

This wasn't much encouragement in itself, but the knowledge that when I finally got to the diner I could have some lunch did sustain me, at least for a while. By the time I was halfway to the diner I felt sure I would never have the strength to make it all the way there. By the time I actually did get there I didn't much care whether I lived or died. And yet I managed to push the Beetle into the car park of El Puerco Loco, and by some fluke positioned it so that the driver's door lined up nicely against the take-out window. The window now opened and a broad, smiling Mexican woman's face appeared.

'The usual, Barry?' she said.

'That's right, Maribel. You know what I like.'

'Yes I do. And how about your friend?'

Through my sweating and heavy breathing I managed to order a cheeseburger and fries. That sounded like a thing a human being might order, though I felt anything but human. I'd have preferred to go inside the diner to eat but I thought it would have been unfriendly to leave my new pal outside, stuck in his car.

While we waited for the food I had to push the car just a little bit farther so that it didn't block the take-out window and it came to rest right next to an out-door table where I could sit and eat, and be in range of the Beetle and its driver.

'I'm Barry,' he said, but I already knew that.

'I'm Ian,' I offered, but he didn't seem very interested. And I thought about explaining what I was doing in Fontinella, my involvement with the movie, my role as writer of the novel, but something told me that a man in Barry's position would be unlikely to be interested. I feared it might sound as if I was just showing off.

In due course our order was ready, and I was reminded how much I enjoyed American food: greasy, salty, sugary and far too much of it. Who could resist that? Barry's 'usual' seemed to consist of everything on the menu – various all-American items but with a distinctly Mexican influence – pancakes, chorizo omelet, a breakfast tortilla, refried beans, and a number of things I couldn't identify. They were stacked up on a tray that I handed to him through the car window. The tray fitted snugly into the angle created by the steering wheel and his large, but yielding stomach.

I sat there at the outdoor table, in that blank, sunless, cheerless spot, eating my cheeseburger and fries, and I have to say I felt perfectly content. It was a blighted spot in most ways, but a writer spends so much of his time all alone in his own room, that to get out, even to a blank, sunless, cheerless spot, sometimes feels like a great treat.

More than that, I reckoned that Barry must be a man with a story to tell. I was a writer who still believed in stories. I thought that hearing this one would be a small reward for the pushing I'd done. But eating and speaking were incompatible as far as my new pal was concerned. He was far from silent, there was much loud chewing, gulping and lip smacking, but no words came out of him. I finished eating long before he did, but I waited patiently for him to ingest the contents of the tray, and then I thought he'd tell me about his life and times. Call me a fool. The moment he was done he said, 'Any time you're ready to push me back is fine by me.'

I could have argued. I suppose I could even have left him there and walked off, and I wasn't entirely sure why I didn't. I suppose it had something to do with retaining my sense of self-worth, of making myself believe I was a decent person, one of the good guys, but as I pushed and strained and sweated all the way back to the speedway gate I had plenty of thoughts that weren't decent or good.

When I'd looked around before, hoping to find someone to help me push the Beetle, there had been no sign of anybody. Now as I entered the gate there was a knot of tattooed, tightly muscled, freakish men standing around sniggering among themselves, and I don't believe it was just paranoia that made me think they were sniggering about me.

I pushed the Beetle back where it had come from, more or less. I didn't say goodbye to Barry, because I was having difficulty both speaking and breathing at that moment. And he didn't say anything either, least of all thanks.

## 9

I arrived back at the gate of Idle Palms to find the same security guard on duty. He was dozing now, seated on a folding stool that I'd have thought provided nowhere near enough support. I gave a nod in his direction, though I didn't expect anything in return, and I attempted to enter the trailer park. At that point the guard burst into life, sprang up from the stool and interposed his body between me and the entrance.

'Yes?' he demanded.

'It's me,' I said.

'That's what they all say.'

'I went out a little while ago. You saw me. You must remember me. We nodded at each other.'

'I don't nod,' he said, and that sounded all too likely to be true. At that moment he didn't look anything like a nodder.

In other circumstances, if I'd been in my own country, if I hadn't still been suffering from jet lag, if I hadn't been on a film set, if I hadn't just been pushing a Beetle and its weighty occupant, I might have been calmer, more tactful, more persuasive and reasonable. As it was, the guard and I began arguing, quietly at first, then louder and louder, and before I knew it I was yelling uncontrollably. I don't remember exactly what I was saying, and I'm sure it wasn't coherent and it certainly wasn't having any useful effect on the guard who was yelling back, just as loudly though with rather less passion. But then I became aware of a third voice some distance away, someone else yelling much louder than either of us, though certainly no more coherently. It was Josh Martin and he was running as he yelled, running across the trailer park, coming straight towards us.

The guard and I fell silent, but Josh Martin did not. He ranted on for quite a while, still not with any great clarity, but we caught his drift soon enough. It turned out he'd been in the middle of a particularly crucial take when we started arguing. The automotive freaks had been paid off, silence had fallen, the actors were at a fine level of creative intensity, the cameras had started rolling and then two fucking idiots had started screaming at each other and their voices were now all over his soundtrack.

'I'm so sorry,' I said, quite genuinely.

'Ah fuck it,' he said. 'Enough of this crap. You're fired.'

It seemed an odd way of putting it. He wasn't employing me, so how could he fire me? Then I realised he wasn't talking to me, but to the guard.

'I mean it,' Martin said. 'You're canned. You're gone.'

The guard straightened up, gained a couple of inches in height and a good deal in dignity, and loped away from his post.

'Josh,' I said. 'Really. You don't need to do this.'

'Don't tell me what I need to do,' Josh Martin said coldly, and then he returned to what was obviously far more important business.

I slunk back to my trailer. I felt as bad as could be. I was a complete ignoramus when it came to movie making, but I knew enough to realise that I had committed one of the crassest, most basic sins: don't go yelling in the middle of a take. I was a fool. I was ashamed. I decided I'd better lie low and stay out of everybody's way for the rest of the day. I couldn't imagine that anybody would miss me. But then, in the middle of the evening, there was a knock on the trailer door that I recognised as Cadence's.

'I heard what happened.'

'Well yes. So did everybody,' I said.

'You shouldn't worry about it. Shit happens. Especially round here.'

'I feel bad about the guy losing his job.'

'That happens too.'

'Yeah, but I was the one Josh was really angry with. The guard just happened to be the one he could fire. It doesn't feel right.'

'Hell, some would say he's lucky to be out of it. Anyway, I thought you might want this,' she said.

It wasn't beer this time, but a large and expertly rolled joint.

'It's called Train Wreck,' she said. 'It seemed appropriate. And it's OK, it's medical. I get it for my migraines. You don't want to buy it on the street. The money goes straight to Mexican gangs.'

It was good stuff, there was no doubt about that, and it should have soothed me, but it didn't. It did, however, put me to sleep, and as I drifted into unconsciousness I realised I'd again forgotten to call Caroline in England. I felt bad about it, but somehow not as bad as all that.

## 10

Another day. I woke early and I didn't even want to
get up. And having got up I certainly didn't want to
leave my trailer and have to face people. I wondered
if there was a possibility of slinking away and
never being seen again. But then Josh Martin was
pounding at my door, and I opened it up and we
looked at each other awkwardly and both said,
'Sorry,' simultaneously, though I did think that mine
sounded a little more heartfelt than his.

'I'm stressed,' he said.

'I was really stupid,' I said. 'My first time on a
movie set and all that.'

He grunted, twitched his shoulders and said, 'Anyway, I've got a job for you.'

Being given a job was obviously better than being
fired from a job I didn't have, though I couldn't
imagine what job he was going to give me. For a
delirious moment I wondered if one of the actors
had fallen ill, or indeed been fired, and that I was
required to step into the breach and perform as a
Volkswagen survivor. It would have been far more
than delirious: I can't act at all, and I know it, but
that doesn't stop me fantasising. Fortunately, for
everyone, all the cast remained in good health and
employment.

'Here,' he said, and he shoved a brown paper bag into my hand.

'Thanks,' I said automatically and I teased open the mouth of the bag to see that it contained a small fistful of banknotes.

'It's not for you,' Josh Martin said. 'I thought that while you're here you should do something useful. A new face might help. Take this money to the freak show. Buy us some silence.'

'All right,' I said.

'Here's what you do. You go over there. You ask for somebody called Leezza. That's with two ees and two zees. You put it right in her hand. She'll do the rest.'

It didn't sound like too difficult a job; or at least it didn't until he added, 'And be careful. Leezza's the only one of them you can trust. Don't let anybody else touch it. Definitely don't let that bastard Motorhead Phil get anywhere near it. And don't get robbed. Don't get mugged. Don't swap if for any magic beans.'

I said I'd do my damnedest not to. I didn't know how much money was in the bag and I didn't try to count it, but it didn't look like a great deal and it fitted easily enough into my jeans pocket. Silence may have been a rare commodity in those parts but it didn't appear to be a particularly expensive one.

I hoped I might borrow the bike I'd seen Cadence using but it wasn't offered, so I set off on foot for the speedway gate, the one where I'd encountered the depressive Barry, and to where I'd returned him. He was still right there: that was no big surprise. And it wasn't any more of a surprise when he beckoned to me again. I had every reason to believe he wanted another push to the diner. I hoped it wouldn't come to that, but I had to talk to him, or someone, if for no other reason than I wanted him to tell me where, and indeed who, Leezza was. He was delighted to do it. The mere mention of Leezza seemed to brighten his whole day.

He pointed out a young woman sitting cross-legged on the ground a short distance away. She looked a lot less freakish than the rest of the people around the speedway. She was fresh faced, scrubbed-looking, and had no visible body modifications. She wore glasses, and had a short shaggy crop of blonde hair, and even though she was wearing camouflage pants and combat boots she still had the air of a librarian who'd dressed for a rough day among the stacks.

I was surprised to see she was sitting there cradling a laptop, tapping in information and scrutinising the screen intently. Everyone else I'd seen from the freak show had been involved in wholly manual, analogue activities. Leezza's back was resting against a vehicle of some sort. I couldn't tell what it was since it was shrouded under a blue tarp, but it looked too long and low to be a Beetle.

'I'm here to give you this,' I said, and I held out the bag of money.

She was slow to look up from whatever was on the screen of the laptop.

'Do you know anything about trajectory physics?' she asked.

'Sorry, no,' I said.

She looked me over and satisfied herself that I was indeed a man who wouldn't know anything about trajectory physics. She held out her hand and took the bag of money.

'What happened to Cadence?'

'Nothing. They just decided to put me to work. I'm Ian.'

She didn't seem any more interested in knowing who I was than Barry had been. And a part of me felt like protesting, insisting on my status, pointing out that I wasn't just some drone or lackey or gofer, that I was actually *the author*. But again I reckoned that might come over as showing off or, more likely, pathetic, like I was trying too hard to impress, and to be honest I had my doubts about whether literary authorship would actually be impressive to a woman who was concerning herself with trajectory physics.

'Well, thanks, I guess,' she said.

'It's OK,' I said in return.

'I'm not really sure it is,' she said. 'It seems, I dunno, kind of grasping. Still, needs must.'

'It's all right, it's not my money,' I said.

That wasn't quite enough to put her mind at rest.

'Think of it as sponsorship of the arts,' she said.

'OK,' I said, though I couldn't see that it made any difference how I thought of it. Her eyes turned back to her computer screen.

'So that's it?' I said.

'Pretty much.'

I had a certain curiosity about the mechanism by which handing money over here produced silence over there, but it was the least of things I didn't understand about film-making, and I didn't want to pry. I didn't want to over-complicate matters: I didn't want to fuck up. And apparently I didn't. Silence was duly produced. I'd had a small success, and one that was appreciated. They had me going over there with money several more times that day. I can't say that, in any sense, I got to know Leezza in the course of these visits, but we did establish a comfortable and friendly working relationship; the kind that giving money to people often results in.

On the third or fourth visit Leezza said to me, 'That was a nice thing you did yesterday. Pushing Ishmael to the diner.'

'Ishmael?'

'Yeah, that's Barry's name, but he doesn't always like people to call him that. Anyway, it was decent of you.'

'I didn't think I could say no.'

'Some would have.'

'If I'd had a car I'd have given him a jump start.'

'Wouldn't have done any good. That car of his needs more than that. Every guy in this place has tried to get that damn Beetle running and if anybody could, it'd be one of these guys, believe me.'

'I see,' I said.

'And you know, they've offered to saw the top off the car so he could climb out, but he won't have it. Says the car's got sentimental value, says it's a part of him. So that's why somebody has to help him get to the diner. Once in a while some of the guys will be going down there anyway and one of 'em'll throw a rope round the front bumper and haul him down, but that gets weary pretty fast. Lot of the guys won't do it any more. They say he got himself into it, he should get himself out of it.'

'I suppose,' I said, 'if they just left him where he was he wouldn't be able to eat and then he'd lose weight and he'd slim down and then he *would* be able to get out of the Beetle.'

'That'd be plain cruel,' she said. 'You're not a cruel man, are you?'

'No,' I said, 'I'm not.'

'You should come over tonight,' she said.

'Should I?' I asked. It wasn't an invitation that I expected or even understood.

'It's opening night. Our first night.'

I looked at her blankly.

'We're a famous automotive freak show,' she said. 'Tonight's the opening night of our new production. There might be a few glitches, but that'll make it even more interesting. Starts at eight. I'll put you on the comp list.'

'Really? Thanks.'

'Sure. Just so long as you give Barry another push to and from the diner.'

## 11

# Linda Lovelace's Veedub Ordeal

When tangle-haired, slack-throated porn star Linda Lovelace meets Chuck Traynor in Florida in 1970 he's driving a Jaguar XKE and she's impressed by that, but the car is only a temporary fixture. Chuck's career as bar owner, drug dealer and pimp is a volatile one, and the day duly arrives when the Jaguar is gone and he turns up to see Linda in an old Volkswagen Beetle. She's less impressed, but she stands by her man and the car becomes far more of a fixture in their otherwise increasingly rickety lives.

Chuck is a restless man. Often he says to Linda, 'Let's go for a ride,' and she says fine, and in she gets and off they go, and she never knows where they'll end up, but that's OK, she likes that. She likes adventure.

One day they're driving all the way from Miami, Florida, to Aspen, Colorado, a tough enough journey at the best of times in any car, but much tougher in an old Volkswagen Beetle without air conditioning. Then Chuck decides he'll make it tougher still and plans a detour to Juarez in Mexico. This surprises Linda a little. Why would they want to go there?

Chuck explains. He's got a plan. Once they get there, he says, he's going to make Linda have sex with a donkey: in public, on stage, for money. On previous evidence he's almost certainly serious about this. The prospect excites him. Having power over Linda excites him even more, and given her endless capacity for compliance she's unlikely to refuse to co-star in this donkey show.

As he drives, Chuck talks about it endlessly. He's obsessed. He's aroused. He starts using the word 'haemorrhage' far too often for Linda's liking, and she starts to wonder if there might be a way out. She prays, asking God to intervene and prevent them ever getting to Juarez.

The next thing she knows they're on the road outside of Little Rock, Arkansas, and Chuck's Beetle is suddenly rammed from behind by a drunk in a station wagon. Chuck loses control of the car. The Beetle takes off, swerves to the right, to the left, across the road and into a ditch. It's a bad crash, but not a fatal one. And as truck drivers descend on the scene and drag Chuck and Linda out of the wreckage she hears one of the truckers say, 'Well, that Volkswagen Beetle has had it.'

Linda is relieved and delighted. Something seems to have been confirmed. She tells herself there may well be a God, or at least some higher power that protects overly compliant porn stars, and intervenes just in time to stop them being fucked on stage by donkeys in Mexico. The universe, she concludes, is not entirely malevolent; just the men she meets.

**12**

I gave Barry and his Beetle another push to the diner. I was doing it to please a woman: how foolish was that? But this time I definitely did want something for my efforts. After we'd got to the diner, after the food had been ordered and eaten, and when Barry was ready to be pushed back to the speedway, I told him I wanted to hear his story, otherwise he and his Beetle would be staying right where they were for the foreseeable future. I hoped this didn't make me too cruel a man.

Barry gave me a suffering look, and yet something suggested to me that he was more than willing to tell all, an intuition that proved to be entirely correct. There were times as I listened when I wondered if the story would ever come to an end, and of course it troubled me that Barry told his story in the third person.

Barry said, 'It's the old story, I suppose: a young man grows up in the north of England – Did you know that I'm English, just like you?'

'Yes,' I said. 'The accent's a bit of a giveaway.'

That wrong-footed him for a moment, as though he thought that until then he'd been successfully passing himself off as an all-American boy. He soon got into his stride, however.

'A man grows up in the north of England. He

becomes a librarian, a sub-librarian, a sub-sub-librarian, actually. The northern town isn't such a bad one for a Volkswagen driver in some ways – a rear-engined, rear-wheel-drive car is very good for the steep hills they have there. Not so good in other ways: bad winters, rain, snow, salt, pollution, football supporters. It eats into you. He feels his fate lies elsewhere.

'He decides he wants to be a road warrior, but it's hard to be a road warrior in England. Actually it's hard being a road warrior just about anywhere but it's easier in some places than others. I reckon China and India are where the road warriors of the future are going be knocking about. But I'm old school.

'So he abandons his dull job and hits the road, Ian, in a customised, if decrepit, Volkswagen Beetle that he names Enlightenment, for reasons that largely now escape him. Far does he travel. Much does he see. He hears the heavy-metal thunder. He goes where the streets have no name, and precious few road markings. He keeps his eyes on the road and his hands on the wheel, *wet* on the wheel more often than not. Sometimes he finds himself unable to drive fifty-five. Sometimes he just shuts up and drives. But before too long he discovers that the M62 is a poor substitute for Route 66. As you would.

'But that doesn't stop him having picaresque adventures. Oh no. Sex and drugs are taken and given. He encounters fellow travellers such as Fat Les the Vee Dub King and an investigative journalist called Renata and a commune of cynical ex-hippies. Ah, where are they now? And he becomes a bit of a cult; not a huge cult, not an evil cult, but you know, a cult's always a cult. And he seems to remember there was a climactic battle with the forces of darkness; but he knows he could be mistaken about that.

'Then, later, there is some business with Volkswagen Beetles that were spontaneously combusting all over England, and a gang of Nazi skinheads with ambiguous sexuality, and the kidnapping of a millionaire Volkswagen collector and a weather girl. There's a rave, there's a VW meeting called Beetle Mecca, a name that seems a little bit dodgy even at the time. An old story indeed. You could write a book about it.

'But in the end he realises it isn't enough. He wants someone to show him the way to Amarillo, to San José. He wants to be twenty-four hours from Tulsa. He wants to see crosstown traffic. He wants to see diamonds on his windshield. He wants to have a windshield. So he moves across the pond, Stateside.

'Another old story. He arrives full of hope and optimism and expectation. He sees a future for himself. He changes his name. He works hard and illegally. He stays under the radar. He lives as honestly as he can. He acclimatises. He finds love: he loses it. He makes a little money, loses that too. He buys a car. Not a Volkswagen this time. He buys American. It's a lemon. He trades up. He gets credit. He thinks he's getting a good deal. In fact he's getting suckered. He gets into debt. It's the American way.

'He stays ahead of the game. Briefly. He tries to live by his own rules. He travels. He goes West. He loves the big skies and the wide-open spaces where a man can find himself. He gets lost. He transcends. He endures. He does one or two things that aren't strictly legal, but he's not a bad man. He fights the law, and it's a split decision. He sees a version of the world. He thinks. He feels. He experiences. He has the occasional insight that you might as well describe as spiritual. Doesn't everybody?

'It doesn't last. He loses his optimism. He loses some hair. He loses his boyish good looks. He gets older. He feels older still. Then he looks as old as he feels. Things falter. He loses impetus. He loses his job, his apartment, his good health. He has no health insurance. He changes his car. He trades down. Once he had something bright and shiny and fast, something with status and attitude and a libidinal *frisson*. Now he reverts. He settles for a thirty-year-old Volkswagen Beetle. He thinks it's what he should have had all along. He thinks a man cannot escape his destiny.

'He finishes up living in his car. That's not so terrible. Many have done it before him, people on the way up as well as on the way down. But he knows he's not on the way up. He's depressed, and that's not unreasonable. It'd be unreasonable to feel any other way. He finds solace where he can: in a bottle, in his car, in the arms of less than willing women, at the drive-thru windows of a thousand and one fast-food restaurants. He eats, he drinks. He's seldom merry. But this is America. Everything is there to help him consume, and consume he does: high calories, empty calories, junk calories, killing calories. He tells himself it's life and life only.

'He's demoralised. He's immobilised. He's close to paralysed. He can't see the road ahead. And even if he could see the road ahead he still wouldn't have the stamina, the driving skills or the gas money to take that road. Que sera sera.

'He gets heavier, denser, broader, lardier. He becomes big as a barn door, bigger than a car door. He has trouble walking, or at least he would if he tried to walk. But he doesn't. He stops trying. He tries to stay exactly where he is. In his car. At last he has some success.

'Of course there are some problems when your car is your home: it's easy to become homeless. You can get towed. You can get totalled, even while you're in the car. He can't leave his Beetle overnight at a garage to be repaired because then he'd be out on the street. So he neglects some basic maintenance. He sits tight. He sits in the driver's seat. The inside of the Volkswagen Beetle becomes his whole world. He likes it there. He feels accommodated. He feels safe. He lowers his sights. He drops his standards. His personal hygiene suffers. He doesn't think so much about washing. He doesn't worry so much about smelling. Why should he? Who's going to smell him? He doesn't get close to people. And toilet arrangements are always tricky when you're living in your car, and trickier still if you never leave it; but he has a lot of time to come up with solutions: tubes, funnels, reservoirs, valves, absorbent pads.

'And then the car falters. Seriously. It becomes unreliable. It becomes a liability. It becomes inert. It becomes a non-runner. He knows that a man without wheels is only half a man. He has wheels but they don't move. Does that make him more or less than half? The party's over. The beast is dead. It's time for all concerned to go to a better place.

'And he thinks yes, OK, it's a time of change, a time to move on, a time to go with the flux. It's time to get out of the car, but he can't, he's too big. He's morbid. He's obese. He's stuck in his shell. The body of the car has become his exoskeleton, his prison. It's a tragedy. It's a travesty. It's a metaphor.

'And then, by hazard, he meets up with an automotive freak show who let him park at the abandoned speedway they've taken over; which is better than nothing, but hardly the answer, not that he can imagine there being an answer. And he thinks that, on balance, in the final analysis, at the end of the road, it really doesn't matter much. Doesn't matter if you have a good car or a piece-of-shit car, if it runs or not. And that's the least of what doesn't matter. Movement, happiness, health, love: there's some of the stuff that doesn't matter at all. And it definitely doesn't matter if you're dead or alive. Not to him, not to anyone.

'So yes, it's the old story, and yes, we all know where it's going to end, and we all know it's not going to end well. The breaker's yard. The scrap heap. The recycling plant. That's the oldest story of all.'

Barry hung his head to let me know he'd finally finished.

'Wow,' I said. 'That's quite a story.'

'I've been rehearsing it.'

'It sounded like it.'

'I've had a lot of time on my hands.'

'I can see that.'

'I try to be media savvy.'

'Yes, I can see that too.'

'So did I give value for money?'

'Yes, yes, you did.'

'You got what you wanted? A story?'

'Yes.'

'Time to push me back to the speedway then.'

'You drive a hard bargain, Barry,' I said, and he didn't disagree.

**13**

That night I felt slightly guilty about sneaking away from the trailer park and the movie set in order to go to the automotive freak show at the speedway, but only slightly. Even if my toing and froing with small quantities of money had redeemed me somewhat, I still didn't feel that I'd exactly been 'embraced by the film-making community'. It was good to have somewhere else to go.

I was impressed and surprised to find that my name really was on the guest list, and a man in the box office – nose-ring, Mohawk, tribal scarifications – welcomed me like I was his long-lost pal. I hurried through the eerily empty parking lot to an equally eerily empty stadium.

The word speedway probably has a different meaning in England than it does in America, but I'd definitely pictured something grander than the reality I now saw. There was a simple continuous oval of tarmac, a racing circuit, but stretches of it were in such terrible shape that nobody in their right mind would have wanted to drive a car around it, certainly not at any speed. Fortunately it didn't look as though anybody was about to do that. Rather it appeared that most of the action was going to take place on a short, straight section of serviceable track directly in front of a block of raked wooden seating, where a makeshift stage had been built. Behind the stage, in the grassy centre of the circuit, a dozen or so of the decrepit Beetles I'd seen behind the speedway fence were now arranged side by side in a straight row, with a ramp at either end.

Things were slow to get going. I think they were waiting for the audience to build, but it never really did. There weren't more than thirty spectators all told, but they (we) were an enthusiastic bunch. There was music provided by someone calling himself DJ Ballard, who had two turntables and a vicious drum machine. He started making noise and a couple of guys on skateboards appeared, and did a few tricks that involved jumping over stationary, then moving, cars. It looked difficult and potentially dangerous but it wasn't all that exciting and there was nothing about it that was consistent with my, admittedly hazy, idea of what an automotive freak show might be.

Things got a bit more freakish when a strong man appeared. He was short, wide, glistening, stripped to a thick waist: a body builder's physique run somewhat to seed. This, if the Gothic letters tattooed on his chest were to be believed, was Motorhead Phil himself. Given Josh Martin's opinion of him, I'd been expecting someone totally monstrous, but this man, at least when seen from a distance, looked benign enough. He certainly did a lot of smiling and waving to the crowd. However, he soon demonstrated his really quite frightening strength.

He began by throwing some car batteries around one-handed as if they were bathroom sponges. Then he grabbed the front end of one of the lined-up Beetles and raised it to head height and held it there effortlessly for a good long time before carelessly lowering it again. It occurred to me that he'd have been the ideal man to have on your side if you were, say, trying to push a Volkswagen Beetle to and from a nearby diner.

Then Motorhead Phil squatted down, grabbed a car engine that happened to be lying around near by, complete with fan shroud and exhaust, and raised it some way above his head before tossing it through the air on to the roof of one of the Beetles in the row, which crumpled like tinfoil.

Finally Motorhead Phil took up a central position on the stage and posed like a superhero as half a dozen members of the crew came up and danced around him brandishing car bumpers as though they were samurai swords. The dancing was pretty awful, but it was soon over. Then the dancers started bashing Motorhead Phil with the bumpers, on the back, across the torso and eventually over the head, and while the bumpers got all bent out of shape, Motorhead Phil remained steadfast and impassive, his face bearing the easy expression of a man who was perhaps being gently flayed with feather boas. You had to be impressed.

Then there was a comedy juggler, as thin, gaunt and wiry as a stick insect, who did a plate-spinning act with hubs caps, then appeared to swallow a couple of spark plugs, though there must surely have been some sleight of hand involved there, and then he inserted a dipstick into his throat, the sort of thing a sword-swallower might do, which was for real, as far as I could tell.

And there was sex of a sort. A heavy, sensual,

bronze-skinned woman in a slither of a bikini lowered herself into a Beetle via its open sunroof. Shortly thereafter half a dozen crew members crowded round the car, each carrying a big blue bucket. They reached into the buckets, and pulled out many, many handfuls of snakes, of varying lengths and thicknesses, and threw them in through the sunroof on top of the woman.

I noticed that one of the crew members was the former Celluloid Security guard, the one Josh Martin had fired the previous day. I was glad he'd found a job. Life's like that, I suppose. The door of security slams in your face; the door of snake wrangling immediately opens.

The snakes did what snakes do, they writhed and wove themselves around the woman's body, and she did her best to make dance moves while sitting in place, shifting rhythmically from buttock to buttock in the car seat. I could definitely say I'd never seen anything like it before, but that didn't mean I particularly wanted to see anything like it again.

Later another woman, thinner, less bronzed, and actually less sensual, appeared bound in a straightjacket. She got into another of the Beetles and assistants fastened the seat belt around her. Doors and windows were shut tight and then, exploiting the Beetle's fame for being waterproof, giant hoses were shoved in, again through the sunroof, and the car began to fill rapidly with water.

There was a lot of thrashing and churning as the Beetle filled all the way to its roof and beyond. The water turned into a bubbling, opaque mass, and you couldn't see what was going on in there, but it went on long enough to make you worry about the fate of the woman inside. And then just when you thought something must have gone horribly wrong, she emerged through the sunroof, free of the straight-jacket and the seat belt, and also free of the rest of her clothes. This was quite the crowd pleaser.

And then, across a not remotely crowded speedway, I saw Leezza, or at least I thought I did, and then I thought no, it couldn't possibly be her, and then I thought yes, it definitely was. There was good reason for my confusion. Earlier that day I'd thought she was out of place among the freak-show crowd, and the parts of the show I'd seen so far only confirmed that; but when I saw her walking across the tarmac there was something about her that seemed very different and very freakish indeed. She was wearing a flame-retardant suit, the kind that racecar drivers wear, but this one had been painted with lurid red and orange flames.

That was a nice little touch, I thought, but there was something about the body wearing the suit that seemed lurid too. Leezza was a slight woman and she had small breasts: I'm a man and a writer; we male writers notice stuff like that. But now she had huge breasts, or at least huge falsies, or the flame-retardant suit did. It bulged out as though it had been conceived by a porn star's plastic surgeon. Well, I thought, porn stars and plastic surgeons know a thing or two about what the public wants; and no doubt a freak show needs all the falsity and exaggeration it can find.

Leezza's image was topped off by a long, red, utterly fake-looking wig: you could definitely have called it flame-coloured. And when I saw Leezza put on a pair of huge wraparound, diamanté sunglasses, the effect, or disguise, was complete; Leezza no longer looked even remotely like herself. No doubt that was all part of the idea, though I was slow to grasp the rest of the idea.

Until then I hadn't noticed that the vehicle I'd seen earlier, the one shrouded in the blue tarp, the one Leezza had been leaning against, was positioned a little way off to the side of the stage. The tarp had been left in place all this time, but now, with some ceremony, a couple of crew members pulled it aside and revealed the machine beneath.

I'd been quite wrong about it not being a Beetle. A Beetle was most definitely what it was, or at least what it had started life as. It was now a vehicle that had been stripped down, reduced to its basics, concentrated, distilled. It was partly a Baja, partly a dune buggie, partly a sandrail, partly a rat rod, and yet it was something quite other than all these things.

Very little of the original was left: no doors, no roof, no bodywork to speak of, although a sleek, pointed version of the distinctive Beetle snout remained in place and a mouth full of vicious teeth had been painted across its very tip. There was just one seat, the kind you might find in a jet fighter, and there was a full roll cage.

At the rear of the thing was the engine, naturally. Clearly it was the usual flat-four, horizontally opposed, air-cooled Volkswagen engine, but it had been decked out with various performance add-ons. I knew enough to recognise twin carburettors, upgraded air filters, an oil intercooler and a stinger exhaust, but there were all kinds of high-tech gadgets clamped around it that I couldn't identify. It looked all business, serious business, disreputable business, but again it took me longer than it should have to work out just what that business was.

Leezza got in the car, looking completely and utterly at home, like she absolutely belonged there, and she started the engine. It was one of the most exciting noises I'd ever heard: not just loud, not just powerful, but truly, scarily elemental. It still sounded like a Volkswagen, but a Volkswagen on heat, on steroids, on hallucinogens, a Volkswagen that was ready to scream the place down. Leezza put the car in gear, gave it a sudden blast of throttle and the machine lurched forward, spun its rear wheels, kicked up its front end and did a gorgeous, dangerous wheelie. I was in love.

DJ Ballard put on what he thought was appropriate music, Van Halen's 'Jump', which I thought was a bit old hat. It was the cue for Leezza to drive the car in a long wide loop, away from the seats and the stage at first, but then she turned, began her approach, and brought the car all the way round so that it lined up with the ramps and the row of Beetles in the centre of the track. When the car was dead straight on to the upward ramp, it began to gather speed. The acceleration was so smooth and controlled that it was hard to tell just how fast the car was going, but you knew it must be pulling some serious Gs, and there was only a fraction of a second between it hitting its spot at the base of the upward ramp and becoming airborne. The car launched itself effortlessly into space.

The flight was long and smooth and very clean.

The car remained straight and level, floating, gliding, mocking gravity. It passed without effort over the line of Beetles and landed on the other side, smoothly, precisely at the very centre of the downward ramp. The body sagged deeply on the rugged suspension, the wheels shrugged off the impact, then the car righted itself and went a couple of hundred yards before Leezza spun it round in a handbrake turn. Some cheap fireworks went off in the grass, and DJ Ballard changed the music to 'Ghost Riding The Whip', which I thought was much hipper.

The crowd, such as it was, cheered and applauded loudly, trying to make up in enthusiasm what it lacked in numbers. And one voice was louder, more raucous and frantic than all the rest. It was Barry. Someone had pushed his dead Beetle into position beside the seats so that he had a good view of the jump, or as good as you could have while trapped inside a Beetle. He yelled until he was hoarse, continuing long after everybody else had gone quiet. There was something manic about his enthusiasm. You would have thought he'd seen a miracle, and in truth we all knew he hadn't.

The stunt had been fantastic in a way, very impressive and obviously extremely skilful. You had to admire the clinical, scientific way it was done, and yet I couldn't help thinking there was something just a little too studied and perfect about it. I didn't know much about stunt driving then, and I only know a little more about it now, and I certainly didn't want to see a terrible crash, yet it seemed to me that a great stunt needed to look riskier, to be a bit more ragged, to steer closer to disaster.

As a way to end an automotive freak show it was curiously sedate, and it had absolutely nothing in common with the image on that painting by the gate, the one that showed the flaming car flying over the bottomless ravine. I couldn't have said I went home disappointed but I was certainly left wanting something more. Maybe, I told myself, that was the whole idea.

## 14

If history has taught us anything (and I know it's a big if, and I'm not sure quite who the 'us' is, but anyway . . . ) it's that bad guys come in all shapes and sizes, and in all manner of disguises. If evil tendencies went along with clearly identifiable markers, such as an ugly physiognomy or a black hat, life would be much simpler. Of course the Nazis made it pretty simple. They wore jackboots, sported death's head insignia, they shouted loudly and unpleasantly in German, they had a dodgy salute. In retrospect even those pre-war Beetle prototypes have a distinctly sinister, satanic look about them.

When I wrote *Volkswagens and Velociraptors*, I didn't want my anti-hero Troy, the character who turns into a little Hitler, then into a bigger one, to be too obviously or primarily a fascist. And I didn't want the allegory to be too obvious. I did make him small and dark and resentful but I didn't want him to be an absolute dead ringer for Hitler. I didn't want to make him a disgruntled ex-soldier or a failed artist. I didn't want to give him a toothbrush mustache. I wanted him to be an Everyman who just happened to turn into a Führer. That's why I made him a used-car salesman, and a very English used-car salesman at that.

So naturally I was curious to see which actor was

playing Troy in the movie. I'd seen the whole cast by now, and there wasn't an obvious Troy among them. There was, however, one guy who stood out from the others because he was so much more glamorous and better looking than everyone else. He was more buff, more golden, more like a star, although you'd probably have said a TV star rather than a movie star. His name was Angelo Sterling and he was curiously ageless: he could have been a young guy with maturity and *gravitas* beyond his years, or he could have been an older guy who'd retained his youthful aura. He didn't look Aryan exactly, though he did have elements of a Viking and a beach bum about him. He was the last person in the world I'd have thought would make a good Troy. Needless to say, he was playing Troy.

'Hi, Ian,' he said, joining me as I was foraging for breakfast next morning. 'I'm Angelo. I'm your Troy.'

We had another one of those conversations about whether or not he was the way I'd imagined my character. I'd have been happy to lie and say he was just fine, but I was too slow, or he was too quick.

'It's OK,' he said, 'I know I'm all wrong for the part. I read the script and I thought, Angelo, there's no part there for you. And I didn't really get the concept. It didn't come alive for me. So I went away and read the book, your book, the original, and then I got it, and I *loved* it, and even though I still didn't see myself as Troy I really wanted to be a part of the project. So I signed on. Just to be involved was enough for me. I said I'd be happy to play some minor supporting role. Anything. But you know, I'm cursed with these pretty-boy, leading-man good looks, and one thing led to another, so here I am, and I'm your Troy. Hope that isn't a problem for you.'

I said it wasn't.

'And, Ian, trust me, the script is changing all the time, and my input is to try to move it closer to your original intention, to make Troy more of an Everyman character. That's what you wrote, isn't it?'

'Well, yes it is, actually.'

I assumed there was a big act going on here, but it didn't seem such a bad act, and it wasn't an unintelligent one. If nothing else, it sounded like he understood what I'd written.

'What did you think of the script incidentally?' he asked.

'I haven't read it,' I said.

'What?' He sounded scandalised, and offended on my behalf, then he had second thoughts. 'But OK, on this picture, yeah, that sounds about par for the course. It's that kind of deal. And maybe you've been spared. Between you and me, there are script problems. From reading your book I can tell you really care about dialogue. Your dialogue really crackles. If there's one thing Josh Martin can't write it's crackling dialogue. Actually that's just one of the many things Josh Martin can't write. Sorry, I don't mean to whine.'

'OK,' I said, and I must have looked worried.

'Look, I don't mean to sound disloyal,' Angelo said, sounding utterly disloyal, 'but the fact is, I'm worried that Josh Martin is seriously fucking up this project. It's running away from him, if it hasn't already. The crew hates him. Most of the cast don't trust him. And God knows how the money men feel about him.'

If I'd looked worried before, I must surely have looked infinitely more worried now.

'Maybe you can do something to help,' Angelo said brightly. 'I don't mean rewrite the whole script, though I'm sure you could if you wanted to, but you know, just talk to Josh a little, be gentle with him, try to get him back on the right track. I'm sure you're really good at that stuff. He's really got to calm down, otherwise . . . '

'Otherwise what?'

'Dude, you're the one with the imagination . . . '

At that moment he struck me as a man who was far too old to use the word dude unironically, but maybe he was being ironic. I hoped so.

Of course, when some alpha male who also happens to be an actor, and a Hollywood actor at that, starts flattering you, you're bound to be suspicious. Naturally I thought Angelo Sterling must have some ulterior motive. In fact that's pretty much how I'd react to anybody who tried to flatter me. I didn't want to fall for this guy's charisma and charm, but equally I didn't want to dismiss him simply because he was charismatic and charming.

Whether I fell for his flattery or not, the news he was delivering about the state of the movie, that Josh Martin was out of his depth, that he'd lost the confidence of his crew and lost control of the production, was pretty devastating. The movie wasn't my responsibility, but it was certainly my concern. If the whole thing was a failure, that wouldn't reflect particularly badly on me, and yet at that moment, having got this far, I realised how very much I wanted the movie to succeed. If there was anything I could do to help, I would, but I wasn't sure there was.

'I can see you're doubtful,' Angelo said. 'Why wouldn't you be? You don't know me. You've got no reason to trust me. I could be trying to manipulate you for my own devious ends. But, Ian, here's a suggestion, if you really want to see the way things are around here, go up to Josh and say, "What about the velociraptors?"'

So I did. It was a good question, and one I'd been asking myself all along. Of course I hadn't expected to see the actual, or fake, critters walking round the set, but I had expected to see some evidence of their, at least cinematic, existence. Even if Angelo had an agenda, and even if it was different from mine, what harm could it do to hear what Josh Martin had to say?

I tried to pick a good moment. It wasn't as if I went up to him while he was in the middle of setting up some fiendishly tricky shot or directing his actors in his some profoundly heart-breaking scene. I found him looking reasonably relaxed, standing by a giant cooler full of soft drinks. He was swigging on a bottle of vitamin water, and we began by having a reasonably civilised conversation about the nature of the light in California. We agreed that it had certain advantages over the light in England. He seemed comparatively happy. He said I'd done a fine job of taking money over to the freak show. I hadn't been robbed or otherwise molested and the silence had fallen as and when it was required. This was all good. We seemed to be getting along just dandy, so I thought it was as good a time as any to ask the question.

I even thought I was being tactful. It wasn't as if I

demanded to know where the velociraptors were and how he was going to make them work in the movie and when. I just said, perfectly casually as it seemed to me, 'So, Josh, what about these velociraptors . . . ?'

And that was enough. That was more than enough. A red tide flooded up through Josh Martin's face, a red mist gathered in his eyes and I wouldn't have been at all surprised if red steam had started spouting from his ears. Yes, there was something comical and cartoonish about the instantaneous way his anger flushed through him and took him over, but that didn't make it any less scary.

He crushed the plastic bottle in his hand, but I felt he'd have been equally able to crush a lump of solid metal, and certainly he could have done some serious damage to any part of somebody's flesh that had come within his range. I made some rapid and decisive moves to make sure I was outside that range. I backed away defensively but he came right after me, not too quickly and not desperately. He had plenty of time: there was something relentless and unstoppable about him. He was coming to get me. And he was yelling something about me being just like all the others, about me knowing nothing, understanding nothing, having no concept of special effects and computer-generated images, no grasp of movie finances, having no faith, no trust, no basic humanity.

I thought this was all a bit much. Some of it was well wide of the mark, and almost all of it was unfair. I'd have been the first to admit that I knew nothing about special effects and computer-generated images, but I didn't think I was supposed to. Movie finances were surely none of my business either. And I certainly didn't think Josh Martin knew me well enough to make any judgement about my humanity, basic or advanced. Still, it wasn't the moment to debate such matters.

I increased the speed of my retreat, moving swiftly backwards in the direction of the trailer-park gate, reckoning that sooner or later I might have to turn my back on my crazed director and make a run for it. There was a new security guard on the gate, but like the previous one he wasn't much interested in what was going on inside the trailer park, just determined to keep people out.

Josh Martin bore down on me. Who knows what would have happened if he'd caught me and set hands upon me? Perhaps when it came down to it he'd have realised it was a bad idea for a movie director to maim the man who'd originated his source material. It would surely have made morale on the set even worse. Or perhaps somebody, an actor, one of the crew, even the security guard, would have stepped in and restrained him. Still, I didn't wait to find out.

I sprinted through the gate and made it into the world outside the trailer park. It was an escape of a sort, but it was a very bleak world out there. Josh Martin shouted after me, 'You can run but you can't hide,' although actually I intended to do both.

Now he came running too. We were both driven by desperate urges: mine to survive, his to hurt. It might have been interesting to find out which urge was stronger, but I much preferred not to. And then I heard the sound of a car engine. It wasn't familiar exactly, but it was certainly unmistakable. It was the stunt Beetle from the freak show, the one I'd seen Leezza do her flying jump in the previous night, and it was now barrelling along the empty road, coming towards me, Leezza at the wheel as before, though no longer in the flame-coloured wig or the big-breasted, flame-retardant suit or the wraparound, diamanté sunglasses.

My guess was that the vehicle was built for straight-line speed rather than manoeuvrability, but even so I leapt out in front of it, and Leezza had the presence of mind and the skill to swerve and slow down, just enough for me to jump in.

If Leezza was surprised by events, she didn't show it. Maybe this was the sort of conflict and mayhem you got accustomed to if you were part of an auto-motive freak show. Or maybe she had a very placid personality. Either way she didn't add to the drama. She put her foot down and we accelerated away, leaving behind in our wake the apparently un-stoppable force that was Josh Martin. There was only one seat in the Beetle so I crouched on the bare metal of the floorpan and held on to whatever bits of welded tubing and bodywork I could find. It was a wild ride, a tough ride, a loud ride, but it wasn't a bad ride.

'Is this thing street-legal?' I shouted above the engine roar.

'Well, it's in the street, isn't it?' said Leezza.

## 15

# The Beetle's Burden

These days everybody seems to know Chris Burden as a big-deal, big-time, serious artist with an international reputation. And he is. But for a long time, as far as I knew, he was just some obscure performance artist who once had himself crucified to the back of a Volkswagen Beetle. The 'piece' was called *Trans-fixed*.

It was created, or at least took place, on 23 April 1974 in a garage on Speedway Avenue in Venice, California. Burden stood on the Beetle's rear bumper and had nails driven through the palms of his hands into the roof of the car.

The Beetle was then pushed halfway into the road and the engine was revved hard for two minutes, so that it 'screamed in pain' at Burden's suffering. Then they turned the engine off and pushed the car back into the garage and decrucified the artist. It was all about the relationship between technology and the body, apparently, though I suspect there may also have been some Vietnam War subtext.

It's one of those pieces that for entirely obvious reasons is far more talked about than seen, and for all the 'documentation' that accompanies the work, art history, unsurprisingly, is a bit vague about the specifications of the Beetle used.

From looking at colour photographs of the event we can definitely see the car was pale blue, a standard Volkswagen colour. Its rear bumpers have overriders, which means it couldn't be earlier than a 1957 model, and the tail-lights tell us that it's definitely pre-1961, which was when the design changed. In other words, Burden was nailed to a car that was at least fourteen years old, possibly a little older. I suppose that's understandable. Nobody's going to hammer nails into their shiny new car. I've not been able to find any information about what subsequently happened to Burden's Beetle.

Actually, it's always struck me that a Beetle is less than the ideal vehicle for a crucifixion. It's too narrow and too curved. You'd be much better off using something like an E type Jag with its long flat bonnet, or even the side of a Volkswagen camper.

And I've always thought it would have been so much more resonant if Burden had been driven around the LA freeways for a few hours, bleeding, in pain, wondering whether he'd been forsaken, getting the backs of his legs burned on the engine lid, and possibly being speared by a Roman soldier and given vinegar to drink. Still, what do I know? And I suppose that's how it always is with performance art; everybody's a critic.

## 16

I had seen next to nothing of Fontinella, but now, still in my precarious position on the floor of Leezza's stunt Beetle, I got the grand tour. It was a flying visit and a mystery trip, and it was taken at a terrifying speed that made it hard for me to concentrate. I saw railway tracks, marshalling yards, every kind of business relating to trucks and cars. There may have been an old main street that was a piece of classic Americana, but I didn't see it. Instead I saw some second-division fast-food restaurants, Mexican super-markets, a surprising number of Thai massage parlours, and quite a few trailer parks that looked far less appealing than Idle Palms. I saw all these things briefly and in a bit of a blur, but I saw them.

Eventually Leezza slowed down and then stopped. We were on the outskirts of the town, in a thrillingly bleak and anonymous bit of territory, a patch of land between an unfenced railway siding, a holding pen for trucks that were being repaired and a disused cement works. Why, I wondered, didn't Josh Martin film here? If you were looking for a post-Apocalyptic landscape this would do just fine. I told myself it was better not to think about why Josh Martin did or didn't do things.

'You're full of surprises, aren't you?' Leezza said.

'Yes,' I agreed. 'Sometimes I even surprise myself.'

'Was that guy really trying to kill you back there?'

'Maybe,' I said. 'He's the movie director so I suppose he can do what he likes.'

'Does this mean you're out of a job?'

'I never really had a job,' I said.

'What? You're like a freelance.'

'You could call it that. I just happened to write the book that he happens to be trying to turn into a movie.'

'You wrote a book?'

She sounded amazed rather than impressed.

'More than one, if you must know,' I said.

'Wow, I didn't know people still wrote books.'

'They certainly do,' I said. 'It's just that very few people read them any more.'

'And sometimes they get turned into movies.'

'Rarely, but yes,' I agreed.

'So you're creative. You're like an artist?'

'On a good day, yes.'

'You know about art and stuff?'

'Just enough to get by.'

'That's good. Your opinion means something. Right. So what did you think of the show?'

The idea that an English novelist's opinion might mean something to a member of an American automotive freak show was flattering yet hard to take seriously. Even so, I wasn't exactly lying when I said, 'I liked it. I thought it was really good.'

'You don't have to be polite,' she said.

'There's no harm in being polite,' I said. 'But I mean it.'

'So what was your favourite part?'

'You,' I said, and this time I wasn't lying at all.

'You were great. That was a quite a jump. This is quite a vehicle.'

'You didn't think it could have been better?'

'I suppose anything can always be better.'

'So how?' she demanded.

I hadn't a clue what to say. Look, I'm a writer, I know all about criticism. I know that nobody who makes art or entertainment or anything in between ever really wants to hear anything other than, 'You and all your works are truly, wholly wonderful.' They don't have to mean it: they just have to say it.

And as for 'constructive criticism', well, there's no such thing; that's like constructive pillaging or constructive carpet bombing. So I had absolutely no intention of criticising Leezza and her act, not in any way, not constructively, much less destructively. And when I said, 'You make it look so easy,' I thought I was delivering a fine and positive, but essentially bland, neutral and harmless compliment. She didn't take it that way at all.

'Damn it,' she said, and she was suddenly very upset. 'That's just what Motorhead Phil keeps telling me. He says I make it look *way* too easy.'

'I'm sure it's not easy at all,' I said.

Leezza slapped her hand against the apex of the steering wheel. For the first time I noticed that the steering wheel was made of transparent Perspex, and that Leezza had the most wonderful, long delicate hands.

'Oh, but it *is* easy,' she said. 'That's the thing. It's just a matter of knowing some math, some physics and a little calculus. You have to know what gravity is, you have to know about velocity, drag and wind

94

resistance. But if you understand them, then you understand everything. After that, anybody could do what I do. If you're in this car, and it's going at the right speed, in the right direction and the angle of the ramp is what it should be, then there's no way the jump can fail. It's inevitable. It's just what happens. It's about trajectory-control theory, a time-order set of states in a dynamic system. It's about the forces of nature, orbital mechanics. It's not about the driver. It's not about me.'

'I see,' I said, and I understood what she was saying, at least I thought I did, that although a car flying through space may appear to be defying the laws of gravity, in fact it's absolutely obeying them. That had a great appeal to it, and that being the case, what I said next seemed thoroughly innocent at the time.

I said, 'Maybe it should be *more* about you.'

## 17

So, later that same day, to my amazement and consternation, I found myself at a hastily convened meeting of the dozen or so core members of Motorhead Phil's Famous Automotive Freak Show. Motorhead Phil was running the meeting, displaying the natural authority that comes with being able to toss Volkswagen engines around effortlessly. In person, off stage, he seemed a gentle enough soul, though I did notice that he was toying with a set of jump-leads, repeatedly snapping the clamps on to his nipples, then unsnapping them again. This may not have been a show of strength *per se*, and certainly it was a bit of a distraction, but it did demonstrate an impressive ability to absorb punishment.

I would surely have felt out of place there in any circumstances but now I was more self-conscious than ever, since the group gathered around me – the tattooed, the pierced, the bodily modified, the tribal, the occasionally hermaphroditic – were all expecting me to come up with some big, creative, artistic idea to make Leezza's jump seem less 'easy'.

This was evidently old ground for them, but for my benefit Motorhead Phil recapped some of the bright ideas they'd had in the past. These all seemed to involve things that threatened both Leezza's dignity and life. They'd considered that she might drive the car naked and/or blindfolded, that the Beetle should actually be ablaze as in the painting, that it should land in a tank of water, that there should be a shark in the water, that there should be a mountain lion strapped next to her in the car. One of the guys still insisted this last was a great idea and he said he knew just where to find a tame mountain lion. However, all these options had, for one reason or another, mercifully, been rejected by Motorhead Phil, whose word was law on these matters. But he and his crew all acknowledged that they still needed something extra for Leezza's performance and I, the creative one, the novelist, the guy who was having his book made into a movie, was allegedly the man to deliver it. This was simply nuts.

Barry was there too, and he was a mildly reassuring presence, a somewhat familiar and not unfriendly face. In fact the whole meeting was taking place next to his Beetle. It didn't seem that he was part of the freak show exactly; it was more that he was regarded as something of a good luck charm or a mascot, perhaps because in some ways, given his story, he was the most freakish of the lot of them. It only made me feel straighter and more boringly normal than ever.

'OK, college boy,' said Motorhead Phil, 'let's hear what you have to say.'

It was some time since I'd been called, or been, a college boy, and coming from Motorhead Phil I reckoned it wasn't altogether a compliment. All eyes were on me, and by now I was extremely nervous, but still, in the way that you sometimes do when you're truly desperate, I did manage to come up with an idea.

'I think one jump probably isn't enough,' I said. 'You see Leezza do the single jump at the end of the show. She does it, and yes, she makes it look very easy and then it's over. What if she did a number of separate jumps at different times in the course of the show? With each one getting longer and longer and more difficult.'

A lot of eyes were on me: some of them dead, some forthrightly hostile. My tongue felt a little too big for my mouth but I kept talking.

'So at the start of the show,' I said, 'she jumps over, I don't know, ten Beetles, then later she jumps twelve, then fifteen, so that it gets harder and harder as the show goes on. And maybe at every show the final jump should get longer still. You could sell it like she's going for the world record.'

Had they given me a couple of weeks, I might well have been able to come up with something better, but in the circumstances what I'd just said didn't strike me as such a terrible idea, not a notion of absolute genius perhaps, but not absurd or ridiculous. I felt very mildly proud of myself. Nevertheless, the silence that clamped itself on the group after I'd spoken was so profound and contemptuous I thought that they, like Josh Martin, might want to kill me.

It seemed that my involvement with things creative had now managed to alienate me equally from the two apparently quite separate and contradictory worlds of movie making and the automotive freak show. Who'd have thought it? Somebody broke the silence by farting. I was pretty sure it was intentional.

'What *is* the world record?' Motorhead Phil asked idly.

'I don't know. I could research it,' I said.

'Nah, don't bother.'

'Scholars differ,' said the man with the Mohawk and the tribal scarifications, the one who'd previously behaved towards me like a long-lost friend, 'but if you said two hundred and fifty feet you'd be near enough.'

Nobody argued with him.

'That's a lot of Beetles,' Motorhead Phil said.

'About fifty sideways; about eighteen end to end, that's if you don't leave any gaps,' the Mohawk man said.

The freak show around me started to get up and wander away; only Barry and I, for different reasons, stayed where we were. I felt terrible. I knew I'd disappointed everyone, but perhaps that was inevitable. They'd been expecting far, far too much from me, hadn't they?

Then from the interior of his Beetle, Barry's voice, sounding somewhat less depressed than usual, called out, 'I've got it. I know what the show needs.'

We all looked in his direction: another Englishman without much grasp of the demands of the freak show genre, you might think.

'Yeah?' Motorhead Phil said.

'*I'm* what you need,' said Barry.

This sounded incomprehensible, if not downright nuts, but Motorhead Phil and his crew were more trusting and accepting than I was. They gathered round once more.

'Go on,' Motorhead Phil said to Barry.

'All right, I will,' said Barry dramatically.

Unlike me, he welcomed the attention that was now coming his way, positively basked in it.

'Well,' he said, 'I think Ian's got a point, and he's not wrong, but he's only half right. He hasn't gone far enough. We'll go further. We'll go all the way. We'll go too far. We'll do what he says, gradually make the line of Beetles longer and longer, but the thing is, I'll be in the line. Me. We'll get somebody to push my car so I'm in there with the other wrecked Beetles. And I'll be the last car in the line. I'll be stuck there. I'll be unable to start the car, unable to get away, unable to get out of the door. At risk. If Leezza screws up and doesn't make the full distance she'll land right on top of me. And I'll be killed. A blaze of glory. A show stopper. Death with dignity. It'll be a real crowd pleaser.'

To me this sounded at least as bad as the mountain lion idea, but Motorhead Phil, for one, seemed to like the sound of it.

'Yeah,' he said thoughtfully. 'I can see it's got something going for it. Thrills, spills, the sense of imminent death, a fat self-loathing guy in a Volkswagen Beetle; it might work. But I still think it needs something else.'

He thought hard, and as he thought he pulled just as hard on a jump-cable that was attached to his left nipple.

'How about this?' Motorhead Phil said. 'Every show, every night, the line gets longer, so the jump gets longer too, so Barry's chances of survival get less and less. However great Little Miss Ballistic here is, sooner or later she's going to screw up and come crashing down to earth, so then she's guaranteed to squash the fat bastard. No offence, Barry.'

'None taken, Phil,' said Barry.

I felt a certain duty to be offended on Barry's behalf.

'Yeah, that's it,' said Motorhead Phil. 'I like it. It's got an inevitability about it. Let's do it.'

The others agreed with him, and obviously there was no arguing about the matter of inevitability, but I couldn't see that necessarily meant it was a good idea.

'Are you really sure about this, Barry?' I asked.

'Of course I am. You know, when I first came to this country I always used to drive like a nutcase,' he said. 'I went too fast, I overtook on blind spots, went round corners on two wheels. I didn't care. But I had a charmed life. I never had a crash. I never spun off the road. A cop pulled me over in South Dakota once, asked me if I had a death wish. I said I did. But it didn't do me any good. Wishing's not enough.

'So then I started eating myself to death, and that's going all right, I suppose, but it's a slow business. I'm sure I've got sky-high blood pressure and that my cholesterol's through the roof, and probably I've got a fatty liver and of course I don't do any exercise so my muscles are all wasting away. But I'm still alive. And really it's a miserable business, believe me. A Volkswagen Beetle that drops out of the sky with a beautiful woman in it and puts me out of my misery. What could be better? Who wouldn't want that?'

I turned to Motorhead Phil. I knew he wasn't exactly the voice of reason here, but as the guy in charge of the show I thought that, if nothing else, he might be dissuaded by legal considerations.

'Won't this be like murder?' I said.

'Murder cum suicide I'd call it,' said Motorhead

Phil. 'But we'll get Barry to sign some papers absolving us of responsibility, and it's not like he's got any family who are going to sue us. And even if they did, we've got no money, so no way are we worth suing.'

So it all came down to Leezza. She'd been silent until now, and I took her silence as disapproval, as resistance. I didn't think she could be seriously considering this homicidal variation on her stunt. She was a sane, sensible, scientific sort of a woman, wasn't she? Surely she'd find this whole idea offensive if not downright wicked. What did I know?

'Are you all right with this, Leezza?' Motorhead Phil asked her.

'If you are and Barry is, then sure,' she said, with all the casualness in the world.

And that was that. It was confirmed that everybody, with the possible exception of me, was all right with it. Motorhead Phil slapped a heavy hand on my shoulder.

'Yeah, you did well, Ian,' he said. 'For a college boy.'

It seemed he now meant the term as a genuine compliment, though a stunt that threatened, indeed eventually promised, the death of a fat man in a Beetle wasn't something I was all that keen to take credit for. And in any case, I thought it might still never happen. Perhaps everyone would sleep on it, feel differently in the morning and have second thoughts: maybe common sense would prevail. Who was I trying to kid?

One small consolation was that I didn't think I'd be around to see it. This was my swansong. I reckoned my days of hanging around the movie set, and therefore my days in Fontinella, were all but over. I had a movie director who wanted to kill me. I knew I wasn't welcome on the set. I needed to get out of there. I didn't even want to go back to my trailer, even though it was too late to leave now. Leezza noticed my reluctance.

'You can sleep here if you want to,' she said.

It was a very nice offer, and perhaps not a wholly unexpected one. It had been a strange day, the sort that brings people together. Leezza and I had definitely bonded in the course of it. I assumed that I was being invited to spend the night with her, but I was wrong about that too.

She pointed to the distant line of non-running Beetles parked in the centre of the speedway.

'Pick a Beetle,' she said. 'Any Beetle.'

## 18

It wasn't the first time I'd spent a night sleeping alone in the back of a Volkswagen Beetle and I suspected it wouldn't be my last, but I was certainly glad that it was a rare and passing condition. It brought home the true unpleasantness, maybe even the horror, of Barry's self-inflicted plight. I could see perfectly well how living in a Volkswagen Beetle full time, being in there all day every day, sleeping there every night, being unable to get out, could drive you to despair and beyond.

I didn't get much sleep, so I was awake very early next morning, when it was barely light. That suited me. Now was the time for me to slink back to the Idle Palms trailer park, which I did. My plan was simple. I'd go back there and gather up my stuff. Then I'd find some way of departing – a taxi, a bus, a girl in a Corvette who wasn't afraid to pick up hitch-hikers. Yeah, right. If the worst came to the worst, I'd walk out of there. Then I'd find my way to a car-rental office; even Fontinella must have such things, surely. Then I'd get myself a car and spend a few days driving around and staying in cool old motels, eating in retro-style diners, living the English tourist's American dream.

Fortunately there wasn't much going on around Idle Palms as yet. The new security guard on the gate was in place, and he recognised me from the day before and waved me in with a sanctimonious and disapproving shake of his head. What had they all been saying and thinking about me in my absence?

I went into my trailer. Packing up my few belongings would take no more than a couple of minutes. There was nobody in the trailer park to whom I needed or wanted to say goodbye. A clean, easy, impersonal departure was all that was required. However, as I hunted around for my dirty socks and clean T-shirts I heard stirrings outside the trailer: voices, the sound of machinery being wheeled around and then a car arriving, Josh Martin's Porsche. I took all this as bad news.

I peered through the trailer window and saw that the moment Josh Martin stepped out of his car, a number of people gathered round him: Angelo Sterling, a couple of other actors, various members of the crew. They looked very serious and determined. This might, perhaps, have been what happened every morning on the set, a simple conference to determine how the day ahead should unfold, but I didn't think that was the case here. This gathering looked far more passionate than most of the interactions I'd ever observed relating to the production of *Volkswagens and Velociraptors*. All concerned were very intense, though not angry, not as yet anyway. When Josh Martin was involved, anger seemed only ever to be half a moment away. For now, however, he was unusually subdued. He was doing more listening than talking. The conversation also involved a lot of gesturing, a fairly general waving of limbs at first, but increasingly fingers and arms were pointed in the direction of my trailer, of me. How did they even know I was there?

After a little more discussion and gesturing, the group began to move as a body towards the front door of my trailer. I steeled myself for what I thought could only be an excruciating exchange, but I decided I'd be ready and waiting for them, I'd stand up for myself, take it on the chin, Hollywood-style, and so I opened the door wide before anyone had the chance to knock.

It's unwise to generalise about writers, but I think we can safely say that most of them don't choose to address amorphous groups of people the way I'd been doing lately. By some bizarre fluke I'd managed to win the respect of the freak-show crowd. The movie people looked like a much tougher audience. I briefly considered what to say. Sorry seemed to be the most important thing.

Angelo was at the head of the group. I suppose natural authority comes with being a tall, blond, good-looking actor just as much as it does with being a freak-show strong man. Angelo saw me waiting on the step, taking deep breaths, looking thoroughly anxious no doubt, and he flashed me a big, bleached smile. I hadn't been expecting that. It didn't reassure me, but I felt sure it was supposed to.

'Ian, my man,' Angelo said, and he held his arms wide open, an embrace waiting to happen. I didn't know what that was all about, so I folded my own arms and ensured that the embrace would have to wait a while longer.

'Ian,' Angelo said again, 'Josh has got something he'd like to share with you.'

I assumed it might possibly be another apology. Josh Martin seemed to have no trouble making apologies but that didn't stop him behaving just as badly afterwards, and that was why I was leaving. I didn't want to go through this again. But he didn't apologise, not exactly.

'Er, don't go, Ian,' he said, flatly.

'Carry on, Josh,' Angelo prompted.

'Er, we need you here,' Josh Martin said. 'The movie needs you.'

He sounded like he was reading from cue cards, and what he was saying struck me as complete idiocy. I was in no way needed. The only useful function I'd performed was taking the hush money over to the speedway. It was a job anybody could have done, and Cadence at least could do it on a bike.

'Listen, Ian,' said Angelo, delivering his own lines with infinitely more conviction than Josh Martin had, 'when a movie starts to go wrong, when it loses its way, then you have to go back to the source, in this case to the book. You need to rediscover why you wanted to make the movie in the first place. You need to fall in love with it all over again.'

This sounded entirely reasonable but I didn't see what it had to do with me.

'Er, Angelo's right,' said Josh Martin.

A few crew members grunted their own awkward assent.

'I'm not sure I'm following this,' I said.

'We want you on the project, Ian,' Angelo said. 'We need a writer. We need you.'

'Really?' I said.

I had never thought anybody in the movies would

ever admit to needing writers. Josh Martin nodded gravely.

'But you've already got a script,' I said.

A choking noise sounded deep in Josh Martin's throat.

'We don't need a whole new script,' Angelo said tactfully. 'But we do need somebody to deliver a serious polish here and there. Some new dialogue. Some scenes to clarify one or two plot points. And who knows the material better than you do?'

'Yeah,' said Josh Martin.

Of course, I was not a scriptwriter, not really, not in any meaningful sense. I had in fact been employed to write a couple of screenplays back in England, but they'd been done for impoverished independent companies. My heart hadn't really been in it, and nobody had ever thought the results were worth filming. My screenwriting credentials were therefore decidedly patchy. However, like many an English writer, I'd often had fantasies about writing Hollywood screenplays, and being paid absurd amounts of money to do it. Naturally the fantasy included the knowledge that my scripts would be endlessly mauled and interfered with, rewritten in the image of the latest bankable leading man, and ultimately made unrecognisable, very probably abandoned, but that went with the territory. Yes, it would be frustrating, yes it would be painful, but I'd do my very best not to become bitter. I'd take this tainted, indecent, plentiful money, and run as far as a pleasant beach house in Malibu, where I'd savour the bitter sweetness of my situation.

I knew that none of those fantasy elements would

come into play if I agreed to work on the script of *Volkswagens and Velociraptors*, least of all the indecently plentiful money, but at least this movie had a considerable likelihood of being made. It was being made already. Somebody wanted my work and they were committed to using it. If I wrote a scene today they could film it tomorrow. What writer wouldn't enjoy that?

'We need you, Ian,' Angelo said. 'We need you bad.'

The people standing around him agreed, even Josh Martin, especially Josh Martin. And I didn't disappoint them. How could I have? I became the new scriptwriter on *Volkswagens and Velociraptors*.

*

That night I finally got round to calling Caroline, my girlfriend back in England. I was able to tell her, not without some irony and self-mockery, but quite truthfully, that I was now a Hollywood screenwriter. She was so much less amused and impressed than I wanted her to be. She said it sounded as though I was being exploited. I said the movies always exploited everybody, that was their beauty. She wasn't sure if I was joking or not, and frankly neither was I.

She asked what I'd been doing in the time when I wasn't working. Not much, I said. 'No trips to Beverly Hills or Santa Monica Pier or the Getty?' she asked. No, I said, I'd just been going to the local diner, taking a drive around the sights of Fontinella. Ordinary stuff. She was again, less surprisingly, unimpressed. I was well aware that I was making no mention of the automotive freak show or Leezza, and

I wasn't wholly sure why. Caroline said it sounded like I was going native. I said I didn't know what she meant by that.

## 19

# The Zander Beetles

To date the avant-garde film-maker Matt Zander has made and released ninety-eight movies, which to the untutored eye might seem uncannily and unnecessarily similar. They all have essentially the same title, *Kafer* – the German word for Beetle, and they are numbered *Kafer 1* through to *Kafer 98*.

Each movie consists of exactly one hundred shots, each shot lasting exactly one hundred seconds. That's ten thousand seconds in total, which, since the movies have neither opening nor closing credits, results in works that are precisely 166 minutes and 6 seconds long.

In the pre-digital age, when the drive bands of projectors were likely to run slightly slow or fast, timing was inevitably a rather more hit-and-miss business. Technological advances have enabled Zander to become more thoroughly formalist.

And in truth Zander began making movies when digital media were unheard of, when videotape was still a novelty. He exposed his first footage in the early 1970s, when he was a very young man, using a Super 8 amateur movie camera.

The story goes that he acquired this camera immediately after he'd acquired his first car, a Volkswagen

Beetle. Taking a few shots of a new car is a common enough thing, but whereas most amateurs would be inclined to do endless pans and zooms, close-ups and action shots, Zander simply set his camera on a tripod and filmed his parked Beetle for exactly one minute and forty seconds, a little less than half the length of a roll of Super 8 film. Eager to finish the roll, he found a neighbour who also owned a Beetle and filmed that for a hundred seconds too. The rest of the film he 'wasted'.

There is no shortage of Volkswagen Beetles in mainstream movies, the most conspicuous and irksome example being the Walt Disney *Herbie* series. Elsewhere Beetles can be found playing significant roles in Woody Allen's *Sleeper*, Richard Stanley's *Dust Devil* and Wim Wenders' *The American Friend*, to pick three more or less at random. Among makers of art films, Zander has claimed kinship with Francis Alÿs, whose *Rehearsal 1* shows a red Volkswagen Beetle repeatedly attempting and failing to drive up a steep hill in Tijuana, while on the soundtrack musicians rehearse some Mexican 'danzon' music.

Having filmed 'still lives', as it were, of those first two Volkswagen Beetles, Matt Zander had found his subject, and he has never found another. His entire oeuvre consists of accumulations of hundred-second shots of Beetles at rest, never in motion.

This may sound perverse and restricting, but even the most casual viewing of Zander's works shows a rigour and a scope that is anything but limited. Over the decades he has been to every continent, to hundreds of cities, to thousands of locations; suburbs and ghettos, parking lots and private garages, rain forests and deserts, scrapyards and war zones, and in each location he has selected a Volkswagen Beetle, set up his tripod, and using ever more sophisticated cameras, filmed it for exactly one hundred seconds.

The reach, the variety, the obsessive quality of his work is extraordinary. In each shot the Beetle remains unmoved, a given, a constant in a chaotic world, a world of untold stories, while around it landscapes change, people and animals wander in and out of frame, smoke or debris drift around the car, gunfire or screams are heard on the soundtrack. Zander's films become melancholy, spiritual meditations on technology, diversity and decay.

He has said he will only make two more films, *Kafer 99* and *Kafer 100*, but nobody believes him. At that point he will have filmed ten thousand Beetles, a good number to be sure, but even allowing for natural wastage, destruction and recycling, that still leaves him with many millions of subjects, many millions of Beetles still to be filmed. Some would say his career might be just beginning.

## 20

So began a short but stable and really surprisingly enjoyable phase of my quasi-American life. Perhaps I shouldn't have been so surprised. I spent the days in my trailer writing. That was good. I liked that. Writing was what I did best. Arguably it was the only thing I did well at all. I was set up with a laptop and a printer, and Cadence became my dedicated, over-eager and really not much needed assistant.

Every day I turned out a few new pages that bore some passing resemblance to the novel I'd written, a lifetime ago, as it now seemed. These pages were rather more closely related to the existing but discredited script which I was now finally allowed to read (it was OK, in its way), and more crucially I wrote scenes that explored the dramatic possibilities presented by a group of Volkswagen survivalists holed up in a trailer park in southern California. It wasn't the worst assignment anybody had ever been given. It wasn't exactly easy but it was work I thought I could do, and I tried hard to accomplish what was required of me.

And now, of course, I had to address the question that had caused me so much trouble: 'What about the velociraptors?' There was still no sign of them anywhere. Well, I was told, first by a chastened Josh Martin, then by a more upbeat Angelo, then by the production designer, that like all the best movie monsters, our velociraptors should exist in the minds of the audience as much as they did on film. Later there would be top-of-the-line special-effects wizardry, and then some computer-generated velociraptors would be digitally inserted into the movie, the exact number of them and the complexity of the scenes being determined by Josh Martin's ability to raise further finance. My job, therefore, I was informed, was to concentrate on the human story, the conflicts between people, the changing alliances, the inevitable sorrows, the unexpected joys, the parallels with Nazi Germany, while still leaving scope for an unspecified number of monsters who might or might not ultimately appear.

My script became increasingly littered with characters saying things like, 'Look over there!' and then peering into the off-screen distance, while other characters reacted with terror or pity or shock or ambiguity, or whatever, to things unseen. The absurdity of the situation didn't escape me, but I've always been able to live with a certain background level of absurdity. That was a big help.

As far as I could tell, things were now going much better on the shoot. The risk of disaster had concentrated a few minds. There was a new energy around the set, and the air of lethargy had lifted. Josh Martin still got angry sometimes, but he no longer got angry with me, and that was a great step forward as far as I was concerned.

My own status on the movie was only vaguely defined, and I thought it best if it stayed that way. Of course, in some ways, I was Josh Martin's boy. He was the one who'd chosen to make a movie from my book. He'd written the original script. He was the ultimate authority. If he hadn't agreed that I should do some rewrites then I certainly wouldn't have been doing them. But equally the very fact that rewrites needed doing only emphasised that his skills weren't all they might have been. I was propping him up. And I wasn't the only one doing that. Everybody was, one way or another. But maybe that's the way it always is on a movie. I told myself I was on nobody's side. If anybody had asked, I'd have said I was on the side of the movie.

I busied myself solving matters of motivation, charting character arcs, wrestling with pressing artistic conundrums such as whether Natasha and Troy should have an explicit sex scene. Everyone thought this was a great if not exactly original idea, but I thought it would be much more entertaining if Natasha had an explicit sex scene with Ronnie the dwarf. This was less well received by everyone, except the actor playing Ronnie.

Otherwise I had to determine whether, as Troy became more Hitleresque, he should grow a moustache (I was against this), whether he should make Nuremberg-style speeches (I was basically in favour, though daunted at the prospect of having to write them, and afraid that long speeches would gum up the movie), and also whether I needed to introduce some new characters. It crossed my mind that the movie could make use of, say, a strong man who could throw Volkswagen engines around, or a woman who could make stunt leaps in a Beetle, but I knew I still had to tread carefully in that area.

116

It was no secret that I'd made friends with the freak-show crowd. How could it have been? But Josh Martin still displayed all his old hostility in that direction. I did my best to bridge the gap between tribes, but Josh Martin remained unconvinced about the freak show's essential benevolence and I didn't put much energy into changing his mind. On the occasions when he and I talked – fewer than you might think – we had other, more pressing movie problems to deal with.

*

My days were full, and by the end of each of them I was ready for a serious break, a complete change. That's when I went over to the speedway to watch the automotive freak show. It was a welcome change from the labour of setting down words. It was as non-verbal and as non-literary an experience as you could get.

Watching the skateboarders, comedy juggling, Motorhead Phil's feats of strength, the Beetles filled with snakes and water, was all very well, but I was only really there to see Leezza's ever lengthening jumps over Barry and his Beetle. At first Leezza accomplished the jumps as easily as ever, but having the jump get longer in the course of the evening added a good bit of suspense and development. I never doubted that she'd clear every one of the Beetles and that Barry would survive, but even so I got very nervous as I watched, and I was always a relieved man when it was over. Then I would go 'back stage', compliment Leezza on her performance, and exchange a few words with Barry. It was actually

117

rather hard to know what to say to him. Was I supposed to be happy for him, glad that he'd survived, or should I commiserate that his existence was being drawn out for yet another miserable day? I did a bit of both. It seemed the right thing to do.

Barry was also keen to talk with me about more general things, to ask how life was back in England. He'd been away a long time. Were there problems with immigration? Was there anywhere to park your car? Would an automotive freak show such as Motorhead Phil's even be conceivable in the old country? I answered yes, no and no, and he took some satisfaction from this. He reckoned he was well out of it.

I was now treated with a lot of respect, maybe even affection, by Motorhead Phil and his crew. It was hard to live with at first. I didn't want to take credit for something I didn't think I'd done – Barry and Motorhead Phil were far more responsible than I was for creating Leezza's new act – but endlessly rejecting and shrugging off the gratitude of people came to seem downright ungracious, so I decided to accept any praise and thanks that came my way. If they wanted me to be 'one of them', to give credit where it wasn't quite due, I was prepared to go along with it. I was even consulted about various new aspects of the performance and did come up with at least one creditable idea.

At my suggestion a hole was cut in the roof of Barry's Beetle, not big enough to constitute a sunroof, and definitely not big enough for him to climb out of, but big enough for the spectators to see more of him, and for him to see more of them and wave a high-five or a clenched-fist salute when he felt the urge. As it happened, it also allowed him to see more of his impending doom, Leezza's flying Beetle passing inches above his head. He liked that, as did the crowd.

That word 'crowd' was justifiable now. From the few waifs and strays who'd been at that first show, the audience was growing exponentially. They weren't the classiest or the most sophisticated audience you could imagine, in fact they were very much the way you'd imagine the people who'd attend an automotive freak show would be.

There were many children, many beer bellies, many incomplete sets of teeth. The folks were loud and good-natured and very glad to be there. Of course, there was something grotesque about their enthusiasm. They were coming in hope of seeing a disaster, perhaps a death, and no doubt every night some of them went home disappointed when Barry didn't die. But even for them, there was always the opportunity of coming back another day when the act would be repeated and the outcome might be more to their liking. Repeat business was the name of the game, Motorhead Phil told me, and business was good. Money was being made. Motorhead Phil's Famous Automotive Freak Show began to get a reputation. It certainly got some publicity.

Stories were written in the local papers. There was word of mouth. There was a powerful online following. A TV news crew came along and filmed parts of the show and interviewed Barry, Leezza and Motorhead Phil. Barry did indeed prove himself to be, as he'd have put it, media savvy. He said that the idea for the jump had come from an eccentric, reclusive (and unnamed) English novelist. Everyone seemed to think that added a touch of class and mystery, and I was very glad to remain unnamed.

Barry also said, and this certainly had publicity value, though personally I thought it was pretty tacky, that there was a deeply sexual aspect to all this. The Beetle represented the phallus, the flight through the air was arousal, the fall to earth and his death was the orgasm. That went down a storm.

On the other hand, another strand of publicity was rather sneery and condescending. There was some tut-tutting about Barry putting his life on the line in this way. 'Are we no better than the ancient Romans?' one article asked. We were not, was the conclusion. And some observers reckoned the whole thing was a sham, that when it came right down to it, if anything went wrong, there was some special release mechanism that would allow Barry to escape and save himself.

There was not – of course – and Barry expressed dismay that the public had become so cynical, although cynicism struck me as the least of their problems. Mostly however Barry was grimly, bravely cheerful. You couldn't have said he was any happier or any less depressed but he was clearly comforted by the belief that his end was in sight. Sooner or later the Volkswagen Beetle in the sky would cease defying gravity, would fall to earth and put him out of his misery.

For her part, Leezza did her level best to make sure it was later rather than sooner. I saw a lot of her in this period. We talked every night after the show. Sometimes she took off the wig and the false breasts, and sometimes she didn't. I was happy either way, and I found her just as attractive in both guises. She was undoubtedly very fanciable and I duly fancied her, but I never really thought I was 'in with a chance'. It was becoming increasingly obvious that we just weren't compatible.

As a writer you try to have as broad an empathy as you can. If you want to make your characters convincing you try to understand the murderer as much as you try to understand the victim, the Nazi as much as the Nazi hunter. Naturally, you don't always succeed, and in a way you don't always want to. To understand all may be to forgive all, and there are certain things you don't want to forgive. And in any case there are always limits to anyone's under-standing.

For instance, I thought I could well understand why Barry might withdraw from the world, why a person might reduce his life to what could be con-tained in a Volkswagen Beetle. It made a sort of sense. I could even, without sharing the sentiment, understand why a man might want to end it all.

In a theoretical way I could also understand why somebody might devote his life to becoming a strong man in an automotive freak show and throwing Volkswagen engines around. If you knew you had that potential inside you, you might well decide you had to take it as far as you could.

What I couldn't understand (and I certainly tried) was what might make you dedicate yourself to pro-pelling a Volkswagen Beetle, albeit a highly modified one, through the air, for the benefit of some promis-cuous crowd. You might not be defying the laws of nature or physics because, as Leezza had explained, that wasn't possible, but you were definitely offending against the strictures of safety and common sense. Why would you do that? The fact was, in the end, I found Leezza, her life, her desires, just plain incomprehensible.

Every time I saw her she was working hard, solving equations, creating animations on her laptop, sometimes just doodling on paper. She would draw parabolas, perfect patterns of rising and falling bodies, Volkswagen Beetles at rest and in motion, that in truth bore very little resemblance to the jumps I was watching every night.

She was also involved with the constant retuning and rejigging of her Beetle, changing its power-to-weight ratio, its gearing, its aerodynamics, the suppleness or otherwise of its suspension. The technical aspects of all this were well beyond my comprehension, whether in trajectory physics or motor mechanics, but I had every reason to believe Leezza knew what she was doing, and the proof of this was there to be seen every night. The line of Beetles grew longer but her jumps got longer still.

Even so, she was also achieving the other part of her mission; it did all look a lot less easy than it once had. There was something more serious and earnest about the way she drove the car. The take off was more violent, the jump less elegant, the landing was sometimes scrappy and barely controlled. It added to the spectacle, and it made the spectators realise that something difficult and dangerous was going on, that something was really at stake, but it also made it even harder for me to watch. At the end of the evening, when the freak show and the jumps were completed,

I would stagger back to my trailer at Idle Palms in a state of exhaustion, and fall asleep the instant I got into bed, knowing that the next day I'd get up and do it all over again.

## 21

Being so fully occupied no doubt made me oblivious to many things that were happening on the shoot. I'm sure there were the usual number of friendships, enmities, crushes, intrigues and what not, but I was just too busy to pay any attention, much less be involved. I still had my suspicions that Angelo might be planning some sort of palace coup, and that Josh Martin might end up as a Mad King in exile, but for now, while we all kept working, that seemed less likely to happen, and in any case I didn't see what I could do about it. I tried to keep my head down, keep out of trouble and keep on writing.

And then one evening, about six o'clock, when I was thinking I still had another page of dialogue in me, trouble came knocking. Josh Martin arrived at my door. Cadence was there in the trailer with me as usual, twiddling her thumbs, trying and failing to be busy, but now she went into action, stapling together some sheets of paper that didn't need any stapling.

'Come on,' Josh Martin said expansively. 'We wrapped early. We should go to a bar. We should drink. We should talk. We should bond. We should bare our souls to each other.'

I feared that Josh Martin's bared soul might be an ugly and dangerous thing, but taking everything into account I decided I might do myself more harm by turning down this invitation than by accepting. I said OK.

'I'll slip away then,' Cadence said.

'No you won't,' Josh Martin insisted. 'You'll come and bare your soul too.'

She giggled girlishly, and I was glad she agreed to come. She would dilute Josh Martin's potent presence, and I suspected that after a few drinks she might prove to have a much more appealing soul than he did. Getting three people in a Porsche can surely never be easy, and I had never actually been in one before, but we managed to fit ourselves in, with Cadence draped, absolutely decorously, across me, and we drove into Fontinella, to a watering hole called a the Nerf Bar, a small, single-storey building the colour of Cheddar cheese. The Porsche looked well out of place in the car park, but then so did anything that wasn't a pick-up truck.

Some plastic letters on an illuminated sign outside the bar announced that this was 'Louie Louie Night'. It took us a while to realise what that meant. As we went in, a small band was already set up in the corner of the bar, and they were playing basic but efficient rock and roll. They were performing 'Louie Louie', a great song in its way, crude, simple, a song that any-body can play, and that anyone can sing along with, at least the chorus; the verses are inscrutable and unintelligible and meant to be that way.

Josh Martin ordered three beers and three tequila chasers and we settled into a corner booth that was upholstered in cherry-red plastic. We were as far away from the band as we could get: not very far, given the size of the bar.

'Do you live with a lot of self-doubt, Ian?' Josh Martin asked me bluntly.

We were straight into the baring of souls.

'Of course,' I said.

'Yeah, I thought so.'

'Doesn't everybody live with self doubt?' Cadence asked.

'I don't,' said Josh Martin. 'Least I didn't used to. Now, I'm not so sure. It's this movie. It's doing it to me.'

'Self-doubt isn't the worst thing in the world,' I said. 'If Hitler had had a little more self-doubt then, well . . . '

'Hitler,' Josh Martin said with feeling and made a lemon-sucking face. Things got no better when he said, 'So how are you feeling about the movie, Ian?'

'I'm feeling good,' I said.

That wasn't absolutely true. In reality I was actually too busy working on the script to have time to consider how I felt about it, but that seemed like no bad thing, and I thought it was best to sound upbeat. I also felt that Josh Martin wanted me to ask him how *he* felt about the movie, but I wasn't going to give him that satisfaction. He'd have to do his soul baring without any prompting from me.

The band continued to play 'Louie Louie': it was a long version. At one point a dapper old cowboy got up and played a hot, country-style violin solo, then a pair of Latina girls sang a couple of verses, very possibly in Spanish. They looked like they were having fun; rather more than we the audience were.

'You don't think maybe there are some flaws in the basic premise?' Josh Martin said, meaning

*Volkswagens and Velociraptors*, not the extended rendition of 'Louie Louie'.

'It's a bit late to think about that, isn't it?' I said.

'Is it?' he said. 'I think about it all the time. I find myself asking where's the art? Where's the poetry? I think that nobody believes in the automobile any more. I think nobody believes in polluting the planet. I certainly don't. I want to be green. I want to do something for the environment. I want to make a difference. I want to reduce my carbon footprint.'

Coming from a Porsche driver this seemed a bit rich. If you were looking for someone with impeccable green credentials Barry was surely your man. He didn't use petrol. He didn't use electricity as far as I could see. He certainly didn't use much hot water. I thought it best not to mention Barry to Josh Martin.

'Well,' I said, 'in the movie there are only about twenty people left on earth so, you know, global warming really isn't that big a problem for them.'

Josh Martin tugged at his hair fiercely to show that this didn't solve his basic objection.

'That's just part of the same problem,' he said. 'Here I am making a science-fiction movie while the world burns. Nobody believes in science any more. Nobody even believes in fiction.'

'I do,' I said.

He ignored me. 'Everybody wants to see movies based on true stories,' he said.

'All stories are true,' I said.

This was a pet theory of mine – everything is true, everything is permitted – but I didn't get a chance to explain it. Without realising it, I must have glanced at my watch.

'Somewhere you need to be?' Josh Martin demanded.

'Yes, actually,' I said. 'But not for a while.'

Josh Martin looked like he was settling in for a long, chaotic night in the bar, and I of course wanted to get to the speedway before too long, to see Leezza doing her jumps.

'What's the big attraction over there anyway?' he demanded.

It seemed like one of those things I couldn't really explain in words.

'You should come along,' I said. 'Come and see for yourself.'

'Fucking freak show,' Josh Martin said. 'Fucking parasites. Fucking scum. Fucking Motorhead Phil.'

The words sounded angry but he delivered them with a profound and unexpected sadness. Something about the very existence of the freak show filled him with a terrible anguish.

'Look, Josh,' I said, 'these people really aren't so bad. They like Beetles. You like Beetles. Isn't that enough for you to get along?'

'Where the hell did you get the idea that I like Beetles?'

'Oh, come on, Josh,' said Cadence. And she placed her hand on his tanned forearm.

'Really? How do you get that idea?'

'Because you're making a movie about them?' I suggested gently. 'Because you optioned the book. Because you wrote a movie script about them. Because one way or another you're spending a fair chunk of your life surrounded by them.'

'Sometimes, Ian,' he said, 'I wonder if you're just

pretending to be very dumb. Or if you're actually very, very dumb indeed. This movie isn't about Beetles any more than *Moby Dick* is a movie about a whale.'

'I know that,' I said.

'It's about passion and obsession,' Josh Martin said. 'The Volkswagen Beetle is a symbol. It can symbolise anything you need symbolising.'

'Yes,' I said. 'I know that. You're quoting my own interviews back at me. But it's also a movie about Volkswagen Beetles. And velociraptors.'

I thought that might get him angry but he just looked at me with disappointment and dismay, and we sat for a while without speaking. It was easiest that way. I listened to the band. I realised we'd been listening to 'Louie Louie' for a long time now. Various musicians had come and gone from the stage, the band had grown and contracted again, someone had leapt up and squawked a free-jazz saxophone solo, a large African-American woman had danced the shimmy, but the song had remained seamlessly, relentlessly the same. It had become a bit irritating.

Josh Martin was irritated too. 'In the old days I'd probably have hit you by now,' he said to me.

These old days he spoke of weren't so very long ago as far as I was concerned, and a return to them seemed perfectly likely, but I needn't have concerned myself. Today he didn't think I was worth hitting. He got up from our booth and walked over to the stage. For a moment, unlikely as it seemed, I thought he wanted to sing a couple of choruses of 'Louie Louie' with the band: stranger things had happened, but that wasn't what he had in mind at all. He tapped the bass player on the shoulder, and as the guy turned his head, Josh Martin swung a wild, loose punch at him. Even if it had made contact it would probably have done no damage; the bass player was squat and solid and looked like he could take a punch, but in any case he rocked back and the blow went right by him. Still, it evidently wasn't a thing that could be ignored or allowed to go unpunished.

The bass player grabbed the body of his guitar and jerked it upwards, quickly, sharply but without much effort, and he used it to deliver a dense, precise upper-cut to Josh Martin's chin. The bass line remained as solid as ever. With a surprising smoothness, Josh Martin's head snapped back and his body followed, a rearward dive, a flop, and he landed full length on the bar's sticky wooden floor. He lay there, ignored by the rest of the bar, and he stayed motionless, inert, looking perfectly, unaccountably content, until Cadence and I started to drag him away. As we made it to the door, an old soak at the bar yelled after us, 'You should come back next week. It's "Wind Beneath My Wings" Night.'

## 22

Driving a Porsche with three people in it, when one of them has passed out and you're the one behind the wheel and you've never driven a Porsche before, isn't easy, but it's probably no harder than being the passenger who *hasn't* passed out. At least that's what Cadence led me to believe. She had to sit on top of Josh Martin as I drove us home. He was feeling no pain, though I guessed he would in the morning.

'I thought you handled him pretty well back there,' Cadence said.

'I didn't really handle him at all.'

'You didn't get angry. You didn't let him get to you. You didn't rise to the bait.'

'The bait wasn't very tempting.'

'Still. It's good that you know how to handle your director.'

'I thought the bass player handled him better than I did,' I said.

We made it back to Idle Palms, managed to get out of the car and to stuff Josh Martin back inside.

'You don't think he's dead, do you?' I said.

'He's just drunk. He's just sleeping it off.'

'He only had a couple of drinks.'

'In the bar he only had a couple. He drinks all day, Ian, every day, or hadn't you noticed?'

'I miss a lot of what goes on around here.'

'I guess you do. So. What now? Want to hang out? We could talk about literature. Or something else. Or we needn't talk at all.'

'I have to get to the speedway,' I said.

'Have to?'

'Well, I want to.'

'But you make it sound like a duty.'

'In a way it is, but like I said to Josh, you could come too.'

'I don't think so.'

'We could talk about literature while we watch a guy throw car batteries around.'

'No. It would seem disloyal.'

'To Josh? To the movie?'

'Yes.'

'It wouldn't be,' I said. 'It really wouldn't.'

'For me it would. It's OK. I'll find something else to do.'

So I went by myself to see the freak show. I preferred it that way really, although if Cadence or Josh had wanted to come I'd certainly have welcomed them. Maybe it was something to do with the high jinks in the bar, but somehow the show seemed a bit lacklustre that night. I wouldn't say it had got boring exactly, but it had definitely become very much as expected. Of course that was partly because I'd seen the show so many times before, but then a significant proportion of the crowd had seen it many times too. Motorhead Phil was now selling season tickets, they were being snapped up, and I was starting to recognise some of the regular faces in the crowd.

After the show was over I went to see Leezza, in the usual way, and told her I thought her performance was great, and I wasn't lying, but I did feel a bit like one of those stage-door Johnnies who turns up every night with a bouquet of flowers and tells the diva how marvellous she was, and he means it all right, but in reality he's far too infatuated with her to have any idea whether she's really marvellous or not.

Afterwards, as I walked back to the trailer park, I had a strange sense of disappointment, of an impending decline. I knew that things couldn't go on for ever as they were, couldn't in fact go on very much longer at all. One way or another, however many new pages I wrote, however many filmic ideas Josh Martin came up with, however many takes and retakes Angelo demanded, the movie would eventually be finished; not finished in the sense of completed, edited, dubbed, released, distributed, given awards and so forth, but sooner or later it would be over, the last shot would be in the can. Then everyone would depart from Idle Palms and go somewhere else to get on with the next phase of their lives. Why did that strike me as so terrible?

And I knew that Leezza's stunt jumps must also conclude eventually. Either the distance would get too long for her, in which case she'd bring the car down on top of Barry, which would be a conclusion of a very specific sort, and one that I dreaded, much as it was what everybody else wanted. Or, just perhaps, there might be a less dramatic outcome. Leezza might change her mind, see sense, bottle out. Or Barry would. Or Motorhead Phil would decide that enough was enough. Or the local cops would decide to close down the show, for thoroughly good, obvious safety reasons.

When I arrived back at Idle Palms that night the Porsche was still where I'd parked it earlier, and I could see that Josh Martin was still in there. Perhaps, as Cadence had recommended, he was planning to spend the night there, sleeping it off. It was a much better and safer option than having him drive back to his house in Los Angeles. The car was parked in the shadows under some trees but I thought I could see some movement inside and the glow of a cigarette or joint. At least Josh Martin was alive, and if nothing else, he'd be well placed to start work in the morning.

## 23

# The Autoerotic Beetle

The *Journal of Forensic Science*, Volume 18, Number 3, July 1973, reports the case of a forty-year-old airline pilot, from Corpus Christi, Texas, who killed himself with his Volkswagen Beetle. It was, as far as we can tell, an accident. It appears that the man was aiming for sexual gratification rather than death, though risk and danger were certainly part of the equation.

The unnamed man left home at 6 a.m. on one of his days off, telling his wife he was going to a remote area to practise his pistol shooting. He was found about an hour and a half later by a passing fisherman who didn't know what the hell he'd found.

The subject was naked and dead, wearing a body harness that was attached via a chain to the rear bumper of his Beetle. The car was not moving even though it was in gear, with the engine running, and the steering wheel was tied up so that it could only move in tight, anti-clockwise circles.

The car was a 1968, 1500 model, one of the less common, though by no means rare, semi-automatic versions that has a gear lever but no clutch pedal. Once the car was in gear and running it would move slowly, relentlessly, in concentric circles. The man had chosen a wide piece of road, an area big enough to accommodate the car's turning circle, which according to a road test in *Autocar* magazine, dated February 1968, would have been 36 feet 7 inches 'kerb to kerb'.

It's assumed that the dead man was using his Beetle as part of an arcane, highly personal, sexual ritual. Having taken off his clothes, used the harness to attach himself to the car, then set it in motion, he would have been forced to run in circles after it; a peculiarly mechanical form of submission and subservience. To end the 'performance' all he had to do was reach into the car, turn off the ignition, and everything would stop. Perhaps he had done this successfully on any number of previous occasions.

This time, however, by mischance, the chain connecting him to the car got caught around the Beetle's rear axle and he'd been 'reeled in', brought down to the ground, then dragged round in circles, unable to reach the ignition key. Even though the chain itself had eventually brought the car to a halt, by then our man was crushed against the rear wing and was dead of asphyxiation.

There are so many ways to have sex. There are so many ways to die. To find a unique way of doing both, and one that involves a Volkswagen Beetle, has a certain bizarre glory to it, though I suspect this was of little comfort to the pilot's widow.

## 24

As usual, I slept badly, and I was woken early by unfamiliar noises outside my trailer. There were unfamiliar noises outside my trailer every morning, but these sounded unfamiliar in a brand-new way. I could hear the engine of a truck, the rattling of a heavy chain, several loud, deep, working men's voices. I got up and looked out to see that a couple of guys were arranging to tow away Josh Martin's Porsche, apparently unaware that he was still sleeping in it.

My first thought was that the car must be in the way of the shoot and that some over-zealous and bloody-minded crew members had decided to move it bodily, but I soon realised these were not our guys. There were two men in overalls who were hooking up the car, and I recognised one of them. It was the man whose CV I knew included stints as a security guard and a freak-show snake man. He was now in the towing business it appeared, and he was being supervised by a slick man in a slick grey suit with even slicker grey hair. The slick man was younger than he looked and displayed less tough authority than he wanted to, or perhaps thought he did, but he would do just fine if you were casting someone as a repo man. Josh Martin's car was being repossessed.

As you would, Josh Martin got out of the car. He

did it rather more slowly than you might have expected, given the circumstances, but possibly that was because he was stark naked. Somehow in the course of the night he had shed his clothes, but being naked wasn't troubling him much. It was troubling the three repo guys a great deal more, and it slowed them down a lot. And when Cadence emerged from the other side of the Porsche, every bit as naked as Josh Martin, things ground to a complete halt.

The basic reasons for Josh Martin and Cadence's nakedness weren't hard to fathom: an old story, an older man and a younger woman, the boss and the intern, a boozy night ending with clumsy sex in the cramped interior of a car. That much was perfectly comprehensible. Why they didn't bother to cover themselves up was far less clear. In retrospect I think Josh Martin may have been having a King Lear moment: savouring being naked, windswept, blasted by fate and the elements, tormented, driven close to insanity; and he was acting out his situation for all to see. What Cadence thought she was up to, I have no idea.

Naked though he was, I still expected Josh Martin to try to stop these men taking away his car. It was what anybody would do. I expected him to reason or cajole, say it was all a big mistake, maybe just get very angry and try to bluster his way out of it. But he didn't do any of that. He was very accepting, very Zen. A couple of burly drivers from the film crew were standing by, sleeves rolled up, all too ready to step in and exchange blows with the tow-truck guys: it would have been an interestingly matched contest. But Josh Martin was having none of that.

'It's OK,' he said calmly to anyone who was listening. 'They're taking my car back because I haven't been making the payments. This is what happens when you don't pay what you're supposed to pay. People come and take your stuff back. Cause and effect. There's no mystery about it. I just can't afford to make the payments. And even if I could, I wouldn't. Any spare money I have is going straight into this movie.'

This was encouraging in one way. It said something about Josh Martin's commitment and priorities. It showed that he cared more about the movie than he did about driving a fancy car. That was surely a good thing, and a pleasant surprise given how negative he'd been about the movie last night. What was troubling was the way he linked these two very different expenses. The monthly payments on a Porsche were no doubt extortionate, certainly by any standards I knew, but compared with the costs of making a movie they were surely small change. The one simply didn't equate with the other. Was the movie really relying on Josh Martin to dig into his own pocket for its budget?

As he himself had so vividly and accurately pointed out, I knew nothing whatsoever about movie finance, but even so, wasn't there some ancient Hollywood wisdom about never using your own money to make a film? And weren't there supposed to be backers, producers, at the very least some shadowy and potentially sinister money men? Weren't they supposed to step in and throw their weight around when things got tough?

It clearly wasn't the moment to ask questions about

these things. The car duly was towed away, Josh Martin shrugged it off, didn't refer to it again, and everybody carried on as normal and we got through the movie-making day.

That night, as ever, I went to the speedway to see the show. And there in the crowd, with Cadence hanging on his arm, was Josh Martin. This was a turn up for the books. He hadn't gone back to his home in Los Angeles after the day's shoot: the loss of his car would have created difficulties there, though surely not insuperable ones if he'd really been determined. So perhaps he simply wanted to stick around and be with his new sexual conquest. Or just possibly, I thought, he might finally have overcome some of his hostility towards Motorhead Phil and the automotive freak show, listened to what I'd said last night and decided to see what it was all about.

In a way it seemed to me unfair that after all the bile and anger he'd spat at the freak show he was able simply to pay his money at the gate and join the crowd like any other civilian. I thought he should have been forced to do penance first. Alas, life doesn't work like that. He and Cadence sat some rows away from me, and I felt absolutely sure they didn't want me to join them, but I kept half an eye on them. Josh Martin seemed distracted most of the time, and he certainly looked drunk, but when Leezza did her jumps he paid serious attention. On the last one he even had his cell phone out and he looked as though he was filming it. I thought that was just plain wrong.

Afterwards, as I was on my way to see Leezza as usual, I heard someone behind me shout, 'Hey, college boy.' It was Motorhead Phil, of course, and he curled a big, overmuscled arm around me as he said, 'We need your creative genius one more time, Ian.'

*

Again I found myself at a hastily convened meeting of the core members of Motorhead Phil's Famous Automotive Freak Show, as they gathered around Barry and his Beetle. It was much the same crowd as before, although there was now a bearded lady whom I didn't recognise from the previous meeting. And once again they were all looking to me to provide some new, inspired idea. Once again I felt sure I was likely to disappoint them.

'Thing is,' said Motorhead Phil, 'this has been going on long enough. Too long maybe. I know crowds. These people are getting impatient. I can't keep 'em waiting much longer. Sooner or later the old whore has to take her panties off and do the dirty. No disrespect, Leezza. I'm talking metaphorically, right?'

'Right,' said Leezza.

'I want the big one,' Motorhead Phil said. 'I want to hit it and quit. I don't want to make my whole career out of this. We've all got other things we want to do with our lives.'

I wondered what kind of second acts there were for people who'd been part of an automotive freak show, but I didn't dare ask.

'We need a climax,' Leezza said, looking at me meaningfully, though I wasn't sure of her meaning.

'We need a big finale, a big bang,' said Motorhead Phil.

Everyone stared at me.

'What? You mean Leezza's Beetle has deliberately to crash?' I said.

'Wow,' said Motorhead Phil. 'That's brilliant. You're very smart, Ian. I knew you were. Why couldn't we think of that? A deliberate crash it is.'

'No, no,' I said. 'That's not what I meant at all.'

'Well it's what you said.'

'But . . . '

I knew it was no good saying, 'But . . . '

'OK then,' said Motorhead Phil. 'So we'll have a big final night, a whole day of festivities, a day when Leezza and her Beetle are absolutely guaranteed to come crashing down on Barry. We'll start out with thirty Beetles in the line, then forty, then fifty, we'll break the world record if we need to, and we'll carry on, however many it takes, however long it takes, until she fails. You all right with that, Leezza? You all right with that, Barry?'

Leezza and Barry, to my dismay, said they were just fine with that.

'But . . . ' I said again helplessly.

It wasn't much of a protest, but it was the best I could do.

'You're not telling me we can't pack 'em in for an event like that?' said Motorhead Phil.

'No, I'm not telling you that,' I said.

'Right then. Next Sunday, it is.'

## 25

So the end was very definitely in sight, one of the ends anyway. Come next Sunday night something would very definitely be over. Death was not an absolute certainty, I told myself. Cars crashed all the time and people walked away from the wreckage, but in this case death seemed to be what everybody wanted. The crowd, Motorhead Phil, Barry, even Leezza, seemed to be in love with the idea, perhaps the reality, of motorised death. It appeared that nothing else would satisfy them.

I found myself unutterably depressed. I sat in my trailer and I tried to write more scenes for the goddamn movie, but that was now impossible. I was all written out. It happens to us all, and to far better writers than me. Somebody else would have to take over and finish the job. It seemed that just about anybody could: Josh Martin, Angelo, Cadence, somebody they dragged in off the street, or the actors could just make it up as they went along. It wouldn't be any worse than what I was now capable of producing.

A couple of days passed. I stayed in my lair. Cadence came by occasionally at first, but then she stopped coming. She'd been given a new job on the movie. She was now Josh Martin's unpaid personal assistant, which she seemed to think was a great step up for her, and it was definitely no skin off my nose. I really didn't care any more. I tried calling Caroline in England but I kept getting her voicemail. It was probably just as well. I had nothing coherent to say to her or anybody else.

There were two untouched bottles of duty-free vodka in my luggage. I'd been saving them, complimenting myself on the restraint I'd shown by not downing them on my first two nights in Fontinella. Now I abandoned my restraint.

I stopped going to the speedway. It seemed redundant now. I knew that the big fateful crash couldn't possibly come until Sunday. I'd be there for that all right, but until then I knew that Leezza's Beetle would be just fine, would continue to carve its neat parabolas through the thick air of Fontinella. I knew she would land safely, and Barry would survive, and it would all mean nothing. They were just marking time, going through the motions, spinning their wheels, waiting for the big final, fatal day.

*

There was a brief, brisk rap on the trailer door, an unfamiliar knock, and when I opened up there was the actor playing Ronnie the dwarf. I realised with some shame that I still didn't know his name.

'I'm outta here,' he said hoarsely.

I didn't know what that meant. Had he been fired? Had he completed his scenes? Was he just walking off the picture?

'I'm walking off the picture,' he said.

It didn't come as a huge surprise. It was more surprising that somebody or other hadn't done it sooner.

144

It was far more surprising that he'd bothered coming to see me.

'Oh well, have a drink before you go,' I said, offering him a shot of the vodka.

'No,' he snarled. 'I don't want to drink with you. You're the reason I'm outta here.'

I knew I had many failings but I didn't think any of them was quite bad enough to make an actor walk off a movie, much less refuse a drink. Had my script-writing really been so terrible?

'I'm sorry to hear that,' I said.

'You can drop the pretence of being some civilised, urbane, literary Brit,' he said. 'You might fool the others, but you don't fool me. I finally saw what this movie of yours is all about.'

'I'd love to know,' I said wearily.

'Oh you know all right.'

'But tell me anyway.'

'These people in the Beetles, they're Nazis, right?'

'Yes,' I said, 'some of them, some of the time.'

I didn't see how this could be a surprise to him. If he'd read any part of any version of the script this would surely have been obvious.

'So the trailer park is like a concentration camp, right?' he said.

That, on the other hand, stopped me in my tracks.

'Oh,' I said. 'I never thought of it that way.'

'You can't fool me. That's how you always thought of it. And the velociraptors are the inmates of the camp. And we all know that the Jews weren't the only people in the camps. There were gypsies and homosexuals, the disabled, the mentally ill – and *dwarves*!'

'Yes, I'm sure that's true,' I said.

'You known damn well that's true. So destroying the velociraptors is the final solution, right. That's how you get your racial purity. And in the real world that plan failed. The Nazis lost. The Jews and the dwarves, some of them anyway, survived. But in your movie the Nazis win. The final solution works! How fucked up is that?'

'No,' I said, 'no, really. That's not what I wrote.'

'What we have here in this movie is a piece of pro-Nazi, anti-Semitic, Aryan supremacist fantasy. And you can count me out. I'm outta here.'

And he was. If he'd stayed I might have taken the trouble to explain that my book was a warning *against* Nazism, that I was on the side of the under-dog, that my heart was in completely the right place, that the Nazis were in the camp just as much as the velociraptors were, that the trailer park didn't actually resemble a concentration camp, that the trailer park setting wasn't even my idea. But maybe I wouldn't have bothered trying to explain any of this to him. Maybe I just couldn't have cared less any more.

*

The night was by no means over. It was late and it was very dark but I wasn't feeling nearly as drunk as I should have been, given the amount of vodka I'd consumed. I sat on the front step of my trailer and looked out into the darkness. I could see a campfire over in a far corner of the trailer park, with a few people gathered round it. I couldn't tell who they were or what they were doing, but I could hear fake, whooping laughter, and every now and again the flames from the fire soared upwards, out of control, as if somebody had thrown a splash of petrol on to it. I heard a dog barking ecstatically, and there was a woman's voice, or possibly a boy's, yelping in pain or pleasure, or both.

Then, in the darkness I heard a scuffling, and then I could see something moving slyly towards me. It was a stooped figure, a man moving unsteadily, almost naked, his body smeared with what looked like engine oil, and with various tools strapped around him like weapons: a spanner, some wire-cutters, a ratchet screwdriver. It was Josh Martin. He was far drunker than I was, and he looked infinitely crazier.

'How's it going, Ian?' he asked, the wildness of his voice quite out of sync with the ordinariness of the question.

'Not so good,' I replied.

'Tell me about it,' he said. 'I mean, don't. Don't tell me. I don't need to know. I'm about ready to call it a day.'

'The movie?'

'Yeah, the fucking movie. My fucking pet project. I just hate it. I hate Volkswagen Beetles. I always will. I always have.'

'I don't think you really mean that.'

'I wouldn't lie to you, Ian.'

He swayed towards me and I handed him the vodka bottle which he swept up in a proprietorial way.

'But you signed up for the movie,' I said. 'You agreed to direct it. You wrote the original script, for Pete's sake. Didn't it occur to you that Volkswagens might be involved?'

'Don't get sarky with me, Ian. Of course it occurred

to me. Of course it fucking did. But I was trying to exorcise my demons, OK?'

'You have demons?'

'Yes.'

That answer didn't surprise me, although how these demons connected with the movie was anybody's guess.

'Volkswagen demons,' he said.

'You have Volkswagen demons?'

'Yes. There. I said it. Happy now?'

'I'm not any more or less happy, Josh,' I said. 'I just wish I knew what you were talking about.'

He looked at me hard, with a stare that oscillated between condescending pity and absolute contempt.

'Sometimes I forget just what a foreigner you are,' he said; then, as if being a foreigner was suddenly a thing in my favour, he slapped his bare chest and added, 'This isn't a suntan, you know? OK? I'm a Mexican.'

He said it as if this were the big 'reveal', the grand, dramatic discovery that would have me speechless with shock and wonder. It didn't.

I said, 'So?'

His being a Mexican meant nothing to me. It was a neutral fact. It didn't ring any cultural bells for me. The only Mexicans I knew were screen Mexicans: Salma Hayek, Eli Wallach in *The Magnificent Seven*, Charlton Heston in *Touch of Evil*, Luis Guzman in *The Limey*, Danny Trejo in just about anything. OK, so not all of these, I was fairly sure, were actual Mexicans, though I'd have been hard pressed to say which were and which weren't, with the exception of Charlton Heston.

148

'You like stories, Ian,' Josh Martin said. 'I got a story for you. It's mine. It's not a bad story. Maybe there's a movie in it. It starts with my parents sneaking over the border with me in their arms. I was two years old. We were as illegal as it gets. The Latin peril. We spoke maybe twenty words of English between us. I was called Juan Martinez.

'My mom got a job as a maid; my dad worked in a garage. He knew about cars. And like any Mexican mechanic he knew all about Volkswagen Beetles. Where he came from it was all Volkswagen Beetles all the time. The taxicabs were Beetles, the police cars were Beetles. Even some of the gangs drove Beetles. Though my dad called 'em Vochos in his lingo.

'And in LA there was always work for a VW mechanic, especially if he was illegal and would work for poverty wages. My dad was a pretty good mechanic, I think. But how would I know? I mean he wasn't some automotive genius, he wasn't in love with Volkswagens, but he cared about doing a good job. He tried not to rip anybody off even when he was being ripped off himself.

'And he learned to speak some English, enough for his work, so he could talk about compression ratios and heat exchangers and distributor caps, though he'd have had a hard time holding a conversation about anything else. Every day he came home late from work, smelling of gasoline, and his hands were black with oil, and there were always VW parts lying around the apartment – hub-caps, carburettors, head-lamp lenses. Guess what? I learned to hate that shit.'

The campfire on the far side of the trailer park

flared up again and a man's voice howled like a cartoon wolf before breaking into laughter.

Josh Martin ignored it and continued, 'And are you surprised if I tell you I had a lousy relationship with my dad? I was smart, and I went to school, and I learned to speak English pretty good, and I wasn't too dark, and although I never pretended to be anything I wasn't, a lot of people could look at me and mistake me for a *gabacho*.'

'A what?'

'One of you. A white boy. An Anglo. And my dad kind of spoiled the effect, you know? It was a problem. So I didn't like my dad. I didn't like him because of what he was. And I didn't like myself any better than I liked him. And I pretty much didn't like the world, didn't like anything, so Volkswagen Beetles were definitely on the list of what I didn't like. But you know, you grow up, you get on with it. And so I left it all behind. I moved on, I got ahead. I stopped being called Juan Martinez. I got a couple scholarships. I made a career in the movies: the immigrant dream. Right?'

'I really don't know,' I said.

'Yeah, I think you do, Ian. And you know, you get older, and I'm not saying you get any wiser, but if you're lucky you get a bit less angry. You decide there are some fights you want to avoid. You decide your life might be better if you could get along with your old man. So I decided I'd try and get reconciled with my dad. Like in the movies. Old story, right?

'But it never happened. He died before we could ever really patch things up. And I can't say that Volkswagens killed him. I can't say that working

150

fifteen-hour days, hundred-hour weeks, for poverty wages, in a metal shed in Echo Park, and having no health insurance was what killed him, but I'm pretty sure it didn't help.

'So we flash forward. And I signed on to make this movie. Didn't just sign on. I developed this movie. I produced this fucking movie. Because I thought I had something to answer for. I thought it might be my tribute to my dad, a way of accepting my past. And you're right, Ian, about the Beetle, the Bug, the Vocho, the Pulguita: it can symbolise any damn thing you want it to symbolise. And for me, I thought OK, it might symbolise father and son, filial love, trans-generational respect, accepting who you are and where you come from.

'And you know, it might. But not here, not now. Right here and now, what we got, this movie, it's a piece of cheese, a piece of *Twilight Zone* crap. It's about Volkswagens and velociraptors. It really is. And that's no fucking good. Fact is, Ian, I hate Volkswagen Beetles now more than I ever did before. And of course I still hate myself, and I'd sure probably hate my dad if he was still alive, but you know what, I hate *you* a whole lot more than I hate anything or anyone else.'

He looked demented. He looked murderous. He looked like he was about to hit me. I could see he was in terrible pain, a wounded animal, not so much King Lear now as one of Dr Moreau's beasts. Are we not Volks? I didn't believe that I was personally responsible for all, or even very much, of that pain, and I thought he had no reason to hit me, but if hitting me would have made him feel better, if that would have made everything all right, I'd have been happy to let him do it. He didn't. He slunk away more beast-like than ever, taking my bottle of vodka with him.

## 26

God knows what time it was when I heard the sound of Leezza's Beetle. My perceptions were a little muddy, but there was no mistaking that glorious noise. I heard it getting nearer then it stopped, just outside the trailer park, by the front gate. The engine maintained its deep, guttural rumble, and I was inevitably drawn towards it. The security guard on duty was asleep, and he wasn't disturbed by the engine sounds, which said a lot for his sleeping abilities, and there was Leezza behind the wheel of her Beetle, bright-eyed, alert and wearing a roughed-up black-leather jacket. She looked the business. I realised how much I'd missed her in such a short time. A few days without seeing her had left me wanting a whole lot more. I ran out through the trailer-park gate to talk to her.

'You haven't been coming to see me,' she said.

'No, I . . . '

'Are you bored with me?'

'No, not bored. I just thought I'd wait till Sunday.'

'You disapprove of me, don't you, Ian?'

'Not of what you are.'

'But of what I'm doing?'

'Of what you're about to do, yes,' I said. I thought there was no point denying it.

'I'm just helping a guy out.'

'Which guy? Phil or Barry?'

'OK, I'm helping two guys out. I'm putting Barry out of his misery. I'm helping Motorhead Phil make a buck.'

Those didn't seem good enough reasons to me, but I knew it didn't matter.

'It's OK,' I said. 'I don't expect my disapproval to make any difference to anything.'

'It makes a difference to me.'

'Really? So what if I asked you not to go through with it on Sunday?'

'Then I'd pretend not to hear you. I'd say let's go for a late-night drive.'

We did. I got into the Beetle. There was a cushion on the floor where the front passenger's seat should have been. It was for me: a nice gesture, a great concession to comfort. Leezza drove us into Fontinella. The town was in a deep sleep by now. We went up and down the empty main drag, and at last I saw the much lauded main street of classic Americana, complete with a couple of diners, a streamlined cinema, a white civic building with stuccoed Greek columns and portico, and then we drove to the outskirts of town, past the closed stores and the open petrol stations.

It might have been described as cruising, one version of one of the dreams, not an original one, regarded as stale and outdated by many people no doubt, and environmentally dubious too, and in the end I wouldn't have argued much with the naysayers and spoilsports. Nevertheless this simple motion, this lived fantasy of being in control while burning up no-longer-cheap fossil fuels, oblivious to the real costs, convincing yourself that you're free –

well that still had its attractions.

We stopped at last in front of a barred and gated government-surplus store. It was painted red, white and blue, and there was a small, plump missile mounted on the roof. Leezza killed the engine of the car. The silence was golden.

'So you're really a big fan of the Volkswagen Beetle?' Leezza asked.

'Of course,' I said. 'I wrote the book, didn't I?'

'Is that what you drive back in England?'

I thought of telling the truth, but the truth hadn't gone down so well when I told Cadence I was a Ford Focus driver. Besides, there was some fun to be had in lying. It required me to make something up, to invent a Beetle for myself, but that was all right; inventing things was what I did.

'It's a 1974,' I said. 'It started out as a 1300. Then I messed with it. Put in a Big Boys' Toys 1641, a hot street cam, twin carbs, polished Scat manifolds, sports exhaust.'

'What colour?'

'White. Just plain white.'

'Body mods?' she asked.

'No,' I said. 'None to speak of. It looks absolutely standard, like a perfectly ordinary Beetle.'

'So, it's like a street sleeper?'

'I believe that's what they call them,' I said.

'Sounds so cool,' she said. 'And it's right-hand drive, yeah? Cause it's English. That must be weird.'

'You'd soon get used to it.'

'I guess you can get used to anything.'

'Maybe you'll see it some time. Maybe you'll come to England.'

'Sounds unlikely,' she said; then, 'You ever had sex in it?'

'Yes,' I said cautiously, 'but I don't want you to think I'm a slut.'

'Why would I think that?' she said.

'But you know, my car has doors and windows and a roof, not like this thing.'

'You're saying my car doesn't provide much privacy?'

'You might as well be doing it in the road,' I said.

'You say that like it's a bad thing.'

Nevertheless she seemed to take my up-tight, inhibited, finer feelings into account. She leaned over a long way and kissed me on the mouth, then restarted the car, slipped it into gear and we were moving again, heading back where we'd come from, towards the trailer park and the speedway. She took some strange back way, along service roads that I didn't even know existed, and she drove us in among fences and piles of scrap metal to a place where she stopped, killed the engine and where we then had a bout of very wild sex.

Sex in an ordinary Beetle is, there's no doubt about it, a tricky, cramped, restrained, inelegant, unsatis-factory business, but in a Beetle that's been stripped down so much that it's ready to fly, well it's a very different matter. I say 'in' a Beetle but that gives a very limited idea of what we got up to. We had sex in it, on it, inside and out, on every surface, lying against it, using it for support, in the driver's seat, on the floorpan, on the boot, on the bonnet, our flesh pressed up against the windscreen, against the wheels, against the non-standard aluminium petrol tank. The car became a fun house, a climbing-frame, an apparatus, a sex aid. The Smut Bug. The Fuck Bug.

And when it was over, and I was wallowing in a sump of warm post-coital pleasure, I became gradually aware of my surroundings. We weren't in such an unfamiliar place after all. We were in the grounds of the speedway, and around us were Beetles in various states of decay. It wasn't romantic, it wasn't secluded, and as I now saw, it wasn't even uninhabited. There, just a car battery's throw away, was Barry's Beetle. And there, in the car as ever, was Barry. He'd been watching us and now he was weeping.

My first thought was that somebody, some joker or pervert or sadist, had pushed his car precisely here so that Barry was in a position where he was forced to watch the dirty (in the best sense of the word) deed. But then I saw it another way. Maybe nobody had pushed Barry anywhere. Maybe he'd remained right where he was, where he just happened to be, and Leezza had parked her car right in front of him. What the hell was that all about? Had she done it by accident or design? It was a very unlikely accident. It was an absolutely incomprehensible and disgusting design.

'This isn't right,' I said, and I got up, pulled on my clothes and stormed away.

'Hey, don't go,' Leezza said.

I ignored her, walked on and she came trotting after me. That was something but not much, and it explained nothing.

'What's going on here?' I said. 'What are you up to?'

'Nothing,' she said. 'At least nothing bad.'

'You once accused me of being cruel,' I said. 'How does it compare with this?'

'I'm not being cruel.'

'I think you are.'

'Then I'm being cruel to be kind.'

I didn't know what she was talking about. I kept walking. She kept coming after me.

'That makes no sense,' I said.

'You don't know the half of it.'

'That's because you haven't told me the other half.'

By now we had gone some distance from the car, from the scene of the crime. We stood there in the dark arguing for a while longer, and then, from behind us, we heard the sound of the engine starting in Leezza's Beetle. You couldn't mistake it. My first absurd thought was that it must be Barry. Some miracle must have occurred. He'd transformed himself. He'd got out of his car. He was free, he could walk, he could drive, and his first action was to steal Leezza's car.

Once I'd dismissed that notion, the reality became all too obvious. The car thief was Josh Martin. He'd been hiding like a predator, lurking amid the cars and scrap metal, waiting for his chance. We'd given it to him. And now he drove right by us, not all that quickly, headlights ablaze, smiling, waving, naked at the wheel of the unfamiliar car, still covered in oil, still conspicuously drunk. The car disappeared loudly into the darkness.

'Oh Jesus,' I said.

Leezza took it very calmly.

'That poor sad fuck,' she said. 'He really doesn't know what he's let himself in for.'

## 27

# The Led Beetle

In March 1938, Bruno Schweizer organised an expedition to Iceland, searching for ancient shrines dedicated to the Norse gods Odin and Thor. Some say he was looking for the Holy Grail.

The trip was organised by a German Nazi group, established by Himmler, known as the Ahnenerbe, or more fully Studiengesellschaft für Geistesurgeschichte, Deutsches Ahnenerbe; in English, the Study Society for Primordial Intellectual Science, German Ancestral Heritage; an organisation engaged in occult research worldwide.

Iceland was a special location for Himmler since he believed it was the birthplace of the Aryan race, with a continuing connection to Thule, the mystical, mythical German homeland. Having not been much invaded over the centuries, Iceland was evidently a place where racial purity could persist.

There's certainly some fun to be had in imagining Nazi occultists thrashing around Iceland in Volkswagen Beetles, perhaps in the military version, the Kubelwagen, or the amphibious Schwimmwagen, which was occasionally converted into a snow vehicle, known as the Schwimmwagen walzen, but as far as I know Schweizer didn't have this luxury. In fact he didn't have much of anything: German currency restrictions hampered, then led to the abandonment, of his expedition.

*

In June 1970, at the early height of their powers, Led Zeppelin's touring schedule took them to Iceland. According to their tour manager, Richard Cole, they were there 'at the request of the British government', as part of a cultural festival.

It would be idle to accuse Led Zeppelin of being Nazis, despite Robert Plant's golden-god status, and Jimmy Page's unapologetic wearing of SS regalia, both in private and public. And it would be equally idle to listen to their music in expectation of hearing joined-up thoughts.

Nevertheless, while on that Icelandic trip they were inspired to write 'The Immigrant Song'. The lyrics, which for sound copyright reasons I shall paraphrase, speak of a 'we' who come from a land of ice and snow to conquer new lands, fill the fields with gore, and become overlords of the world while singing, 'Valhalla, I am coming.' If this isn't pernicious Aryan claptrap then it will certainly do until the real thing comes along.

Unlike the members of the Ahnenerbe, however, Led Zeppelin's Icelandic expedition was well funded and certain members did have a Volkswagen Beetle experience.

*

The notion that a Volkswagen Beetle will float on water may well come from the war years, when Allied forces first encountered the Schwimmwagen. But ordinary Beetles do indeed float, and can be made quite seaworthy. I've seen modified Beetles at car shows that have chugged quite happily across open water, and a man called Malcolm Buchanan once crossed part of the Irish Sea from the Isle of Man to the coast of Cumbria in a Beetle.

And Volkswagen themselves, or at least their advertising agency, have exploited the myth. A print ad from the 1960s shows a Beetle floating in a tank of water with the caption, 'Volkswagen's unique construction keeps dampness out'. A man in a television ad proclaims, 'It's so well put together it's practically airtight,' and then drives it into water, where it does indeed float, at least for a while.

Having a bad-boy, hell-raising image to live up to, certain members of Led Zeppelin – John Bonham and John Paul Jones, along with tour manager Cole and a roadie – rented two Beetles, one green, one white, and after a certain amount of alcohol and boredom had set in, they decided to see whether there was truth in this advertising.

They found a river and Bonham, with Jones as his co-pilot, powered the white Beetle off the bank, through the air and on to the water. To their considerable surprise the car really did float and remain watertight, for about two minutes, and then water started to seep in around the bottom of the doors. In fairness, the ad never said how long a Beetle would float for.

It couldn't have been very dramatic, and Bonham found the experience rather enjoyable. Jones however was furious. As he explained when he got back on dry land, a fan had given him some grass the previous night and he was keeping it in his sock. The water ruined his stash. What a complete tool. What an unconvincing story.

## 28

We came out of the east, driving into the sun, a horde if ever I saw one, not that I'd ever really seen one, and only if a horde can consist of about thirty people in about a dozen Volkswagen Beetles. We were a ragged, miscellaneous band in their equally ragged, miscellaneous rides. We had all the cars that had been built for the movie, plus the ones from the automotive freak show that Motorhead Phil's crew had been able to patch up and get running in quick order.

We looked scary. That was the idea. The people from the freak show could look effortlessly scary at any time, and the actors had decked themselves out in their survivalist drag from the movie. There were also some angry crew members to whom Josh Martin owed money. In their way they were the scariest of the lot.

We looked dangerous, too, and that was at least partly because some of the Beetles were so barely roadworthy that they seemed likely to lose a panel or a wheel or a transmission at any moment. We looked like trouble. We looked like something you'd want to avoid.

Even I looked somewhat scary. I'd been supplied with an outfit: a sheepskin waistcoat, worn bare-chested, and a flying helmet and goggles. I felt like a fool and a fraud, but I also thought I looked pretty cool. The effect was undercut, however, because I was riding in Barry's Beetle along with Barry, an unhappy pairing after the night of Beetle sex, voyeurism and tears, but there wasn't much either of us could do about it.

Of course Barry had to come along. How could he not? How could he be left behind at a time like this? So they had winched him and his dead Beetle on to the back of a flatbed truck and the truck came along too, bringing up the rear, like the final float in a parade, or possibly like a caboose. You could have argued that the flatbed was an inauthentic touch, a seriously un-Beetle-esque item, and I can see your point, but I think you can overdo the quest for authenticity.

I had finished up in Barry's Beetle because I'd been too slow to claim a place in one of the others. It had been quite a scramble, and as ever, notions of hierarchy had been much to the fore. Motorhead Phil, naturally, was in the lead car, along with two of the sensual freak-show women: the snake lady and the underwater-straightjacket woman.

The actor playing Ronnie the dwarf hadn't gone away after all, it turned out, and he was riding along with the actress playing Natasha, a contrasting pair that worked equally well on screen and off. Angelo Sterling was also towards the head of the pack, in a black Beetle convertible, a nice touch that allowed his hair to flow freely behind him like a golden wave. He wasn't driving, however. Leezza was in there with him, a pairing that made me much less happy, although by now my happiness was not on anybody's agenda, not even my own.

There had been much talk before we left about the

terrible things that could and would be done to Josh Martin once we found him. Some were crudely physical, involving punching, kicking, gouging and fracturing. Others were more ambitious and creative: crucifying him, harnessing him to the rear bumper of a Beetle and dragging him round in circles.

Barry and I did our best to be civil in the course of our ride together. We could hardly ignore each other, given the enforced proximity caused by the amount of room Barry took up and the little left for me. There was also the clutter of Barry's life, a limited life to be sure, but one that certainly left its traces. In addition to the evidence of heroic eating and drinking there were numerous books and motoring magazines, and many sheets of paper, some with handwriting scrawled on them, Barry's work no doubt. I glanced at some of it, and although much was illegible, the bits I could make out looked like ramblings, or at least quotations, about Volkswagen Beetles. I spotted something about 'a managerial Volkswagen'. I was hardly surprised. What else was he going to be writing about?

There was an inevitable coolness between us, but that didn't stop Barry talking.

'Some people might say this Beetle is half full,' he said. 'Others might say it's half empty. But I say it's both, simultaneously. Which it is. Obviously. Right?'

'Right,' I agreed, though I didn't particularly.

Then he said, 'I always knew that *vagina dentata* would spell trouble.'

'What?' I said.

'That thing painted on the front of Leezza's Beetle: the teeth, the hole, you know?'

165

'Isn't it just a mouth?'

'Just a mouth?' said Barry. 'Don't be naïve. It's a *vagina dentata* if ever I saw one, and I knew no good would come of it. But I suppose it's easy to be wise after the event.'

'You know,' I said, 'this whole thing about the *vagina dentata* has always struck me as pretty weird. Yes, I can see you wouldn't want suddenly to discover teeth in a woman's vagina, but that's mostly because you're not expecting them. If they were there the whole time you'd soon get used to it. Men don't find the teeth in a woman's mouth much of a deterrent to putting their penis in there, do they?'

'The chance would be a fine thing,' said Barry.

I thought it best not to be too sympathetic.

And later Barry said, 'I know what you're thinking, Ian, you look at me and think there but for the grace of God go I. But you see, here's the thing, God doesn't have any grace. Because it's in the nature of being gracious that you don't hand out the grace unequally. If you're only gracious to some of the people some of the time, then you're not really gracious at all. I'd expect God to know that.'

'I suppose you're right,' I said.

It didn't really amount to conversation. And, of course, we didn't discuss the really important matter of how we both felt about the sexual shenanigans that had gone on last night. Perhaps neither of us knew how we felt. I spent a lot of time looking out of the car window and finding that a lot of people were looking back. A few of the looks were admiring, most of them confused. Somewhere along the way a cop on a motorcycle spotted us and drove alongside for a couple of miles, observing us carefully, but he didn't pull as over. I didn't blame him. If you'd been on the freeway and encountered thirty or so Beetle freaks and their cars in full post-Apocalyptic finery, I believe you'd have thought that letting them go on their way unmolested, to do whatever the hell it was they were going to do, would be the very wisest course of action.

We drove along Interstate 10, the western end of a road that could lead you all the way across America. The sun shone, the air was sparklingly clear. Talk of the famous Los Angeles smog seemed much exaggerated. And then we were in the outlying sprawl, then within the boundaries of the city itself, and on the Hollywood Freeway. Even the name had an excitement about it, though in itself I don't suppose it was so very different from any other bit of American freeway. And although it was nice to think of ourselves as warrior outlaws, we still got stuck in heavy traffic like everybody else. We got even more looks then.

And eventually we saw the freeway exit signs for Sunset Boulevard and then Hollywood Boulevard, which sounded pretty romantic, and then the exit we were taking, called Gower Street, which sounded a good deal less romantic, but it happened to be the one that was most convenient for getting to Josh Martin's house.

I knew he lived in the Hollywood Hills, whatever those were, and we had every reason to believe he'd be at home that afternoon. Somebody in the production office had intercepted some faxes from Josh Martin's lawyer. These weren't absolutely explicit

167

but they referred to some vital and complex financial, legal proceedings that required him to be at his house at four o' clock that day. It all sounded extremely serious, a matter that even Josh Martin in his current state couldn't and wouldn't ignore.

*

I don't know if you've ever driven on the roads around the Hollywood Hills. I haven't – I've only been a passenger – but I imagine that if you had a small, fast, nippy, European sports car with fantastic acceleration, braking and road holding, then you could really enjoy yourself going up and down the fantastically steep gradients, around the tight hairpin bends and terrifying blind corners. You'd flash by hedges in full flower and by palm tress and banks of escapee cactuses, and every now and then you'd find yourself on a crest and get a view right over the city, not that you'd be able to stop and appreciate the view because you'd be concentrating too hard on your driving.

If you weren't in a small, fast, nippy European sports car, but rather in a convoy of Volkswagen Beetles or, say, in a car on the back of a flatbed truck, the ride would be a lot less fun, but that wouldn't stop you seeing the possibilities.

Fortunately Angelo knew his way around these parts – we certainly would have got lost otherwise – and we found our way to Josh Martin's house with only a few hairy moments, when we encountered oncoming pick-up trucks or postal vans, the drivers of which, understandably, weren't expecting to encounter the likes of us.

Josh Martin's home was a perfect little Spanish-style house, with a series of red-tiled roofs, arches and rustic shutters. It was, no doubt, a pricey house, but it wasn't a mansion by any means. It wasn't opulent or showy. Unlike the man himself it was restrained, modest, discreet. There were a couple of expensive cars parked outside, but unless Josh Martin had mysteriously acquired these on his way home, they had to belong to visitors. There was no sign whatsoever of Leezza's Beetle.

Our arrival was loud and hardly unnoticeable but nobody came out of the house to see what the hell was going on. We would have to make the first move. There would undoubtedly have been some satisfaction in seeing all the Beetle freaks marauding through Josh Martin's house, casually destroying things as they passed, and there was every possibility that it might come to that, but initially the majority of the horde stayed outside, forming a guard of honour, while Motorhead Phil, Angelo, Leezza and I made our less grand entrance.

The front gate was unlocked and as we went inside we could hear voices coming from around the side of the house. We followed the sound and stepped on to a green, shady, screened patio. There was a gaudily tiled fountain burbling at its centre, and next to it a stone table at which Josh Martin sat, alongside a man and a woman, each wearing a severe black suit, and together the three of them were perusing a pile of legal documents, and Josh Martin was signing his way through them.

He looked rather better than when I'd last seen him. He had his clothes on for one thing, and he'd managed to wash off most of the engine oil, at least from the areas that showed. I couldn't have sworn that he was stone-cold sober but he appeared more composed and in control of himself than he had been in a long time.

He looked up at us without surprise, and said insultingly, 'Ah, the help has arrived.'

'Any trouble from you,' said Motorhead Phil, 'and we'll turn your house into an architectural junk yard.'

Josh Martin looked casually at the document currently in front of him and signed it with a quiet flourish.

'Not now you won't,' he said. 'It's not my house. Not any more.'

There was a set of keys on the stone table, and Josh Martin now pushed them across to the black suited woman, who took them sadly, earnestly and handed over a legal document in return.

Josh Martin said, 'These good people from the mortgage company are now the owners of this property. They've very kindly offered to let me lease back the place at a very reasonable rate, but since I don't have any money whatsoever I can't do that, which leaves me homeless. I guess there's a trailer park in Fontinella where I could stay for a while, but you know what, pretty soon the owners of that place are going to find out that I'm broke too. They haven't been paid, and they're not going to be paid, and then it'll be truly over and all I'll be left with is part of a movie that I can't afford to shoot or finish or edit or anything else. Welcome to Hollywood, guys.'

This was not what we'd come to hear, and Motorhead Phil and Leezza weren't even interested, but as far as Angelo and I were concerned it was quite the revelation, far more than the discovery that Josh Martin was Mexican.

All too guilelessly I asked, 'But what about the movie's backers?'

'There are no fucking backers, Ian. There were *potential* backers once, for a while, but in the end they didn't back me. They backed out. They were wise, much wiser than me. They saw it wasn't going to work. But I thought hell, fuck it, live the dream, remortgage your house, make the damned movie, *will* it into being and then everything else will fall into place and everything'll turn out just fine. Big mistake.'

Angelo and I were left quite speechless. My stomach descended to knee level. I felt giddy with confusion and disappointment, though not quite disbelief. But Motorhead Phil still had plenty to say.

'Where's the car you stole, Josh?' he yelled. 'Where's the fucking Beetle?'

'The car, yes,' Josh Martin said. 'El vocho volante,' and he laughed, and the laugh was too theatrical for my tastes, or do I mean too filmic, trying to be a little sinister, a little insane, a little superior. Trying too hard. It was certainly a laugh you couldn't trust. It was a laugh that could very easily get you beaten up.

'I'd had a couple of drinks last night,' Josh Martin said.

'That much we know,' said Leezza.

'Mistakes were made.'

'You crashed the car, didn't you?' said Motorhead Phil with disgust.

'Not crashed it, not really, no.'

'You'd better tell me what the fuck you're talking about,' said Motorhead Phil.

'I will, Phil, I will. You see there's an old Mexican saying that those who don't know history are doomed to repeat it. And that's supposed to apply to all kinds of history: personal history, movie history, whatever. But I don't believe it. I think the opposite is true. I think all too often those who know their history *want* to repeat it.'

'This better start making sense soon,' Motorhead Phil said.

'It does. It will. It makes perfect sense, Phil. You see, everybody who's ever seen *Bullitt* wants to race a Ford Mustang through the streets of San Francisco. Everybody who's ever seen *Pulp Fiction* wants accidentally to blow somebody's head off in the back of a car.'

I thought he might have a point there.

'Now I'm not gay, Phil, and I know this sounds a little weird, but the truth is I really like a good Doris Day movie. My favourite? *The Thrill of It All*. 1963, Universal, directed by Norman Jewison; Carl Reiner wrote the screenplay. You know why I like it? Because James Garner drives his car into a swimming pool, and you see . . . '

He was going to tell us more, but there really wasn't any need, and he was interrupted as Motorhead Phil got a thrill of his own by decking Josh Martin with a simple, single, strongman's knock-out blow to the side of his head. I had a feeling it was what Josh Martin wanted.

We ran round to the back of the house where the pool was. It wasn't nearly as big or as fancy or as blue as the pools you see in movies, though it was in every sense a Hollywood swimming pool. And there at the bottom of it, proving that the legend about floating Volkswagen Beetles was, at least sometimes, untrue, was Leezza's submerged, waterlogged, earth-bound Beetle.

*

The guys who knew about these things, Motorhead Phil's technical crew, said the situation was retrievable. The car wasn't heavy: a small crane could be hired to fish it out of the pool. With a bit of careful manoeuvring it could be put on the flatbed truck next to Barry's Beetle. Then it could be taken back to Fontinella, stripped down, dried off, reassembled and it would be as good as ever by next Sunday, and then Leezza could do her jumps exactly as planned. Most of this proved to be true, but not all. There was one small hitch.

The crane was brought, the Beetle was hooked up, and they were soon putting the sodden, dripping, streaming thing on to the truck. Leezza, very concerned, a little tearful and very hands-on, was squatting on the flatbed, peering closely at the underside of her car, trying to see what damage had been done when the car went into the pool. Quite a lot it seemed to me. One of the tyres had burst, the trans-axle was askew and all the basic geometry of the chassis looked out of whack. Leezza was very close indeed to the car, too close, as we now know. While she was inspecting the damage, the crane driver, unaware of where she was and what she was doing, dropped the Beetle the last twelve inches or so on to the truck, and the front right wheel, the one with the burst tyre, landed directly on top of her right foot. If the tyres had still been inflated it surely wouldn't have been too bad, and obviously it could have been a lot worse, but as it was, the solid metal of the wheel hub and the flattened rubber smashed down against Leezza's instep, shattering three of her metatarsals. It would be a good long time before she was able to walk or drive again.

## 29

Transvestism is a tricky word, a tricky concept and, as I now know, an even trickier reality. There's no denying that as I put on Leezza's flame-red wig and her flame-retardant suit with the big false breasts sewn inside, I did feel some *frisson* of transgression. I can't say there was any sexual pleasure in that, in fact no pleasure of any kind, but I certainly did feel that I was doing something wrong.

I also found it hard to believe that I made a convincing woman. My gait and posture were surely all wrong and I thought the wig only made my features look even more angular and masculine. Still, as Motorhead Phil told me, red hair and big boobs broadcast a loud, clear message that tends to drown out the background hum of more subtle, more telling signals. He assured me that by the time I'd put on the crash helmet and the diamanté wraparound sunglasses, the crowd (none of whom was going to get near enough to inspect me and question my gender assignment) would be seeing me as all woman.

This made him much happier than it did me, and I didn't altogether believe him. I was also a little concerned about the ethics and potential consequences of trying to deceive a large, volatile, paying crowd of automotive-freak-show enthusiasts, but the truth was I had far bigger things to worry about.

Leezza's Beetle would no doubt have felt awkward and unfamiliar in any circumstances – it was built specially to fit her – but operating it while wearing these odd items of feminine disguise presented a whole other set of problems. I was very glad indeed that Leezza's outfit didn't include high heels, hot pants, thigh boots or any of a thousand and one other possible female accessories.

I'd had only the very briefest amount of time to get used to the car. Predictably, the drying out and reassembling had taken much longer than predicted. I'd driven the Beetle just a few times around the lumpy, crumbling circuit of track at the speedway, but I hadn't as yet made a jump. The one I was about to undertake, in public, in front of a crowd, 'on stage' as it were, would be the first of what I, and everyone else, suspected might be a very short series.

The freak show, I had been told, must go on. A broken foot, even Leezza's broken foot, was no reason to stop the fun. The main *reason* the show had to go on, however, was because Motorhead Phil had sold an amazing number of tickets for the final Sunday, and it wasn't in his nature to give refunds. As far as the audience was concerned the entertainment would be going ahead exactly as planned and advertised. A sexy red-headed woman would be jumping her car over Barry and an ever-lengthening row of Beetles, right up until the moment when she didn't. Replace 'sexy red-headed woman' with 'overwhelmingly nervous English novelist' and that was what they were still going to get.

I had been chosen to impersonate Leezza because . . . well, not for any good reason that I could fathom, since there were surely people attached to the auto-motive freak show who had some experience of these things, certainly more than I did, since I had none whatsoever, but Motorhead Phil said I had to do it because the whole thing had been my idea. I knew that wasn't true, and I did protest just a little, but Motorhead Phil was a hard man, an impossible man, to argue with. Given that I had none of Leezza's skills or experience, the event did promise to be a good deal riskier, and perhaps more exciting, and far more likely to end in failure, although by this time, notions of success and failure had become im-possibly confused in my mind.

I sat in the car on the speedway's tarmac, and I tapped the accelerator lightly, revved the engine just a little. Even through my terror and cold sweat it sounded great. It was fiercely, violently responsive but not out of control. It was a beast you could do business with even if you couldn't fully tame it, and when it came down to it, why would you want to? Its wildness was its attraction. It was ready to rock, ready to race, ready to soar, far readier than I would ever be, but our fates and our destinations were now absolutely connected.

I tried to remind myself of all the things Leezza had told me over the last few days. She had been my mentor, my driving and flying instructor, and if I was a slow learner, I was also – in the interests of self-preservation if nothing else – a studious and deeply committed one. And above all else I told myself what Leezza had insisted on from the beginning, that this whole thing wasn't personal, wasn't about the person in the car. It was about forces in motion, about the laws of physics and gravity, of trajectory mechanics. If you understood those and went along with them, the outcome was guaranteed.

It all sounded like perfectly good advice, in a way it even sounded reassuringly like common sense, but there was still the question of whether my alliance with these timeless, immutable, non-negotiable laws was all it needed to be. I had a pretty good idea of what I was supposed to do: what had to be done. I knew, at a theoretical level, all about the required speed, about the direction, the angle of ascent, about the required rate of acceleration, but I still had actually to do it. If I did it wrong, if I lost my bottle, well that would be the moment when, instead of the show being about immutable laws of nature, it would become all too much about me. And about Barry, too.

The speedway was packed. The crowd was excited and loud and beered up. Motorhead Phil made some kind of announcement over the PA. I wasn't really able to listen, but I could tell it went on much longer than it needed to. DJ Ballard was manning the decks and was playing something he thought appropriate: could it have been 'Moby Dick'? 'You Are The Wind Beneath My Wings'? 'Love Lifts Us Up Where We Belong'? I couldn't make it out, and I didn't try too hard. I had other things to do.

I put my foot down and the Beetle seemed to crouch, to sink into the ground and grip it with a positive, feral firmness, and then the car surged forward. The process had started. We were on our way, and there was no coming back. I knew the car was moving incredibly fast, and yet I had little sense of the vehicle itself. The world had turned into motion blur, as if I was being sucked into the pinched mouth of a circular tunnel. Ahead of me there was an eye of clarity, the take-off ramp, my target, and everything else was out of focus, forcing me to concentrate on the bull's eye ahead. It looked perfectly still, and of course it was, even though it was approaching so rapidly, or rather because I was approaching it.

I felt an unexpected coldness right in the middle of my chest as though someone was pressing an icy fist into my solar plexus, and my flesh and bones were too soft to resist. Nobody had told me about that. It was strange and scary but it wasn't altogether unpleasant, and it was definitely a distraction, and then . . .

. . . and then I was off the ramp and airborne and I felt, well I felt a great many things, most of them oblique and ambiguous, but the main one was relief. Look, I wasn't a complete idiot; I didn't think that nothing could now go wrong, or that I'd achieved anything that could be called 'success', or that all my problems were over, but at least, at last, the dice were cast. I was no longer responsible. I was no longer even trying to stay in control: other forces had taken over. What would be would be. To be airborne at all was such an achievement. Whether I landed nose first or arse first, regardless of what those vaginal teeth painted on the front of the car sank themselves into, whether I crashed and burned, literally or metaphorically, at least I'd made it, however briefly, however incompetently, by whatever fluke, into the air. That was something. That was a lot.

A screaming came across the sky. It was the sound of an air-cooled, flat-four, horizontally opposed Volkswagen engine. But now it was an engine without

179

purchase or purpose. It was the power behind a falling Beetle. The car was out of its element. Its wheels were spinning but only in air. It had some velocity, some thrust, some momentum, but it was only a pre-destined dying fall. It was on a one-way trip, down to earth, and I was nothing but a passenger.

There was no road noise, no tyre squeal, none of the reassuring sounds of contact. You couldn't have called it quiet, you couldn't have called it peaceful, but for a moment there I was suspended in a little cone of what felt like stillness and was in reality rapid forward motion.

And although my time in the air was minimal, a second or two at most, I still had the leisure to notice, to discover, with amazement rather than pleasure, that another set of mechanics (fluid, I supposed, and popular too) were obeying their own laws inside my body, inside my blood, and as I savoured my disconnection from earth, a dense and serious erection asserted itself between my legs, inside my feminised flameproof suit. Nobody had told me about that – Leezza probably didn't even know – but it did suggest that Barry had been on to something when he said there was a deeply sexual aspect to all this.

I'd been warned not to do anything dramatic while the car was in the air, that anything I might be inclined to do, either out of panic or dumb instinct, things like slamming on the brakes or yanking the steering wheel, would either do nothing or might lead to disaster. I had even been warned not to look down, and from up there, with the sunglasses and the crash helmet and the fake red hair falling over my face, it was hard to see much of anything. Even so I did direct my eyes downwards and I became aware of rapid, purposeful activity on the ground, some people running towards the line of Beetles, some running away from it. I could only have guessed what was going on down there, and I had no time to guess.

I crashed. Of course I did. How could anyone ever have expected me to do anything else? I was an amateur, a novice, a virgin, an incompetent. What else could I have done? I was obeying the laws of nature, of my own nature too.

But I didn't crash all that badly. I didn't crash lethally, and I didn't crash on top of Barry and his Beetle. In fact I came nowhere near him. There were thirty Beetles side by side in the line for that jump, Barry in the thirtieth of course: we were nowhere near any version of the world record. And I cleared nine of the thirty with complete ease. That was surely a cause for celebration. If you'd told me a couple of weeks earlier that I'd be jumping a car over nine Beetles, or eight, or actually even one, I'd have been amazed and thought you were crackers. Jumping over nine Beetles was surely not something to be sneered at.

However, as is the way with these things, the problem was Beetle number ten. You might say that numbers eleven to thirty were all problems as well, but most of them were problems I never actually encountered. I didn't get that far. I crash-landed inelegantly, ineptly, yet surprisingly safely, on top of the tenth Beetle, a bright orange saloon with its windows already busted out. And of course my car's momentum guaranteed that I made a pretty ugly mess by smashing into Beetles number eleven, twelve and even thirteen.

For a while, quite a long while, my world was a chaos of crashing, sliding, buckling, uncontrolled air and metal, but in the end, in the very end, eventually, inevitably, everything stopped. The series of impacts and ricochets, actions and counteractions came to a halt. The flying Beetle and I were still, grounded, and if not entirely intact – and I was certainly in better shape than the car – then at least we hadn't been utterly destroyed.

I waited anxiously, not daring to move, scarcely daring to breathe, expecting something else to happen, a climax, a petrol leak, flames, an explosion, a stroke, a heart attack, but nothing did. Guys came running, some bearing a stretcher and some with fire extinguishers, but they weren't needed. I needed nothing at all. I was OK. I hadn't died. That seemed rather important to me at the time. And I obviously hadn't killed Barry: in a way that was more important still. I hadn't done precisely what I'd set out to do, I hadn't done what people wanted me to do, what people had paid to see, but I'd done something very important: I'd survived. There was plenty of satisfaction in that.

I stood up unsteadily in the car, holding myself up on the roll cage, and I waved to the crowd. There was a little bit of booing, but less than you might have expected. Yes, some of them were disappointed, they hadn't been given exactly what they were promised, but they'd seen something that wasn't such a terrible approximation. They'd seen a flying Beetle, a crash, a red-haired, big-boobed woman waving to them. Wasn't that enough?

Leezza's car was a terrible mess, a wreck; there

would be no subsequent jump. I was delighted. My nerve had held once, I wasn't sure it would have held again. But some people's nerves, I discovered, hadn't even made it through that one jump of mine. I looked along to the end of the row of Beetles, in Barry's direction, towards the thirtieth car. I thought a wave, a shrug, a handshake, maybe an apology, would have been in order. But I couldn't see Barry. There was a scrum of people around his Beetle but he was not in it.

The story, which it took me a good while to work out, was as follows. Both Motorhead Phil and Barry had, in a strange sort of way, more confidence in me than I'd had in myself. They really thought I was going to clear all the Beetles except one, that I was really going to fly over twenty-nine cars and descend precisely on top of Barry. As my Beetle, Leezza's Beetle, had approached the take-off ramp, Motorhead Phil couldn't stand it any longer. He'd panicked, rushed across the track to Barry's car, used his incredible strength to pull off the driver's door and then, Samson-like, tried to push apart the sides of the doorway to create a large round hole, big enough for the equally large round Barry to escape through. Motorhead Phil made the hole all right, but his efforts were wasted, superfluous. Barry too had cracked under the strain. Suddenly he wanted to live, he wanted it very much indeed, and he decided to make his own way out of the Beetle. For one reason or another – depression, increased metabolism caused by all the excitement and anxiety, loss of appetite caused by pining for the faithless Leezza – he had lost some weight. This, plus a steely determination

183

to escape and a previously unimagined ability to compress himself, meant that while Motorhead Phil was demonstrating his strength on the driver's side of the car, Barry was able to kick open the passenger door and squeeze out that way.

I wasn't sure whether to feel flattered or insulted by their estimation of my driving skills, but either way, I could see they had a point. As Barry so eloquently put it, 'It's one thing to be crushed to death in a Beetle by the woman you love, but being crushed to death in a Beetle by an English novelist in drag – gimme a break.'

**30**

It's six months later, and I'm back in California. It's only temporary. I haven't gone native, despite what Caroline might say. I've been home; I've been getting on with my life. I've been writing. But suddenly here I am again, on a movie set, specifically on a full-scale sound stage in Burbank. It's very different from Fontinella in some ways, not so different at all in others. Chiefly there is a great deal more of everything: more people, more lights, more cameras, more activity, more commitment, more expertise, more money, more free food, more *stuff* of every kind.

Oh yes, and there are velociraptors, lots of them everywhere: models, puppets, animatronics; velociraptors made of rubber and foam and plastic, with metal armatures and ingenious, magical remote-control mechanisms. The creatures come in various sizes and varying degrees of completeness, sometimes there's just a head on a stick, sometimes a single clawed foot or just an evil, beady glass eye – whatever's required for their use in a specific scene or shot in the movie. This makes me happy. This feels like real progress.

But exactly as in Fontinella there's an awful lot of waiting for something to happen; more than ever, a lot of standing around being sort of interested and sort of bored. Right now, for instance, we're waiting for a Volkswagen Beetle to be filled with cement. Really.

*

The truth is, everybody who's ever owned a Volkswagen Beetle has got a Volkswagen Beetle story. 21,529,464 Beetles: that's a lot of stories. And some people have owned more than one Beetle. Some people have owned fleets of them. Some people have *collected* them. And that's why some people have multiple Volkswagen stories. Our job is to cash in on that.

Anything that can be done in, on, with or to a Beetle has been done. The cycle of conception, birth and death, even burial, even resurrection, has been played out around a Beetle; old stories, of love and hate, loss and redemption, fire and ice and explosion: archetypal stories, movie staples. It all adds up to a lot of history, and as Josh Martin so very nearly said, whether you know it or not, you're always guaranteed to be repeating some version of somebody's history. Certain people may even feel the need to repeat somebody's urban legend.

Jan Harold Brunvand, the author of *The Vanishing Hitchhiker*, the first great book about urban myths, what they mean and how they spread, details several clusters of Beetle-related folklore, including 'the cement-filled Beetle'. In this story a man who works as the driver of a ready-mixed-cement truck is driving past his own home one day and spots a Volkswagen Beetle parked outside. He recognises it as belonging to a friend of his. He parks the truck, goes into the house (very quietly, if the story is going to work) and finds his wife and friend in bed together, too engrossed to notice the husband's presence. He slips out of the house without disturbing them, fills the Beetle with liquid cement from his truck and drives away. By the time his friend has finished in the bedroom the cement has solidified and his car now weighs several tons and has to be towed away by a special, heavy-duty tow truck.

As with all urban myths, this one comes in multiple versions, and moves effortlessly around the world – the United States, England, Denmark, Kenya – changing its specifics with local circumstances. Norway has a surprising number of variations. Sometimes there's an extra twist: the friend and the wife aren't in bed, but sitting innocently on the sofa, nevertheless the truck driver jumps to the same conclusion and again fills the car with cement, only to discover that wife and friend were in fact planning a surprise party for him. Sometimes he fills the car without even going into the house, and then discovers the wife won it in a competition or bought it for him as a birthday present.

Sometimes, to be fair, the car isn't even a Beetle, and becomes something far fancier and more expensive, making its ruination that much more magnificent, but this also tends to make the story less believable. The fact that the Beetle is so ordinary and ubiquitous, helps with the credibility of the myth.

Ultimately, after much careful research, Brunvand concludes there's no evidence that the events in the story ever happened at all, anywhere, to anyone. But that doesn't make the story any less significant or potent as a myth. On this movie set, on this sound stage in Burbank, California, however, the cast and crew of the revivified production of *Volkswagens and Velociraptors* are about to make it happen 'for real'.

*

It feels good to be back in California. I couldn't exactly say that I feel at home here, but certainly my actual home in England, in rural Suffolk, seemed extremely tame and grey after the dramas I'd been through in Fontinella, and the writer's life, back at my desk, back at my computer, seemed especially plain and uneventful. Doing spellchecks and word counts, you'll be unsurprised to hear, doesn't contain quite the same raw exhilaration as launching a Volkswagen Beetle into the void.

I didn't bother to tell people back home much about what had happened to me in Fontinella. Of course I told them that the production had ended in chaos, that Josh Martin had been a crazy man, that it had all been insane and unsatisfactory, but I didn't tell the half of it. I didn't mention my involvement with the automotive freak show, and I very definitely didn't mention my brief, tarnished moment as a transvestite stunt jumper. I didn't even tell my girlfriend Caroline about that. I thought it would sound either too fantastical, like I was making it up, or worse, that I was boasting.

Before the cast and crew of the movie went their separate ways, we all exchanged email addresses and promised to keep in touch. Nobody from the automotive freak show made such promises, and naturally nobody from the movie kept in touch with me, but after a month or so I did get an email from Angelo

Sterling with a link to an online news item about a dead body that had been found in the burned-out wreck of a stolen Volkswagen Beetle that had spun off the road and ended up at the bottom of a canyon some way north of Los Angeles.

At that moment Josh Martin was still missing in action and Angelo thought it might be him. I had my doubts. It seemed too neat, a little too laden with poetic justice. And for what it's worth, I was right. A week later I got another email from Angelo. They'd identified the body as that of a former security guard and tow-truck operator, though they didn't mention his brief career as a snake wrangler, which I thought was a shame.

And shortly thereafter Angelo did manage to track down Josh Martin, who, as it turned out, despite being broke, was alive and in some ways perfectly well, and with Cadence's help was in the process of reinventing himself as a maker of music videos for Latino rap bands. I learned this in another email from Angelo, but I didn't read much into it, even though he told me I should stand by and 'await developments'.

And then I got a very unexpected phone call from him. The production of *Volkswagens and Velociraptors* was suddenly back on, he said. He'd been busy. Having found Josh Martin he'd made him an offer he couldn't, and certainly didn't, refuse. I wasn't party to the fine print of the arrangement, but I think Angelo must have agreed to pay off some of Josh Martin's debts, and in exchange he took over ownership of the movie.

It sounded like a pretty good deal for Josh Martin,

though far less good for Angelo, I thought. I couldn't see that *Volkswagens and Velociraptors* was anything worth owning, but what did I know? The next thing I heard, Angelo had managed to find backing from one of the mini-major studios and then we were back in business. Well, I wasn't, not really, not personally. Grateful though Angelo was for all the work I'd put in revising the script, he was taking the movie in a different direction. He'd written a new draft of the screenplay, and although it was very different from the novel, it was, he said, completely faithful in spirit. He thought I'd be very happy with what he'd done. He was now writer, producer, star and director of the movie. I guessed it was what he'd always wanted. He said I should come out for a week, visit the set, maybe bring my girlfriend, come and see that not all movies were made the way Josh Martin tried to make them.

*

And that's why, in the loose company of a lot of other people, I'm standing here in Burbank, on the sound stage, waiting for a Volkswagen Beetle to be filled with cement, a scene that bears not even the slightest resemblance to anything that happened in my original novel. That's all right by me. I have no false pride, not much real pride either. We're in the world of illusion, naturally, and it comes as no surprise to learn that the car here is not really being filled with real cement. They're using some kind of lightweight, silicon-based, non-setting, but nevertheless utterly convincing, substitute. They have experts who specialise in this stuff and make it look authentic: nice work if you can get it.

In fact there are now video clips on the web that show what actually happens when you fill a Beetle with cement. Nothing at all happens for quite some time until the tyres blow because of all the increased weight, then the windows pop out from the internal pressure, and then cement flows out through every seam and crevice of the car; slowly at first, then very rapidly. It's sort of interesting though it's really not all that exciting.

But this is the movies. This will be far more dramatic, more visually intense, far cooler. I know this because I've seen the storyboards. This movie Beetle, which isn't a real Beetle at all of course, just a prop, just a construct, will fill up like a balloon. Tyres, windows and windscreen will remain miraculously intact, and the car will bulge, expand, become stretched to breaking point, until it is close to spherical. There will be all sorts of tension. Then the car will explode, violently, disastrously, but gracefully, in ultra-slow motion, seen from multiple angles by multiple cameras. Cement and Volkswagen components will then fly in all directions, carving parabolas of glittering, spinning debris and light as they're propelled from the centre, expelled outwards, falling with infinite, balletic slowness, each following its own natural trajectory.

And then, just when things are starting to settle, from the centre of the explosion, from the heart of the remains of the exploded Beetle, a figure will very slowly emerge, a man, a man covered in glop, his features and body caked in cement substitute, but even so you can see he's no ordinary man. He is a big man, strong, dense, heavily muscled, a mountainous monster of a man, and if you know your freak-show personnel you will certainly recognise him as Motorhead Phil. He looks good. He's been working out a lot. The muscles are bigger and more pumped, the bulge that used to be around his waist is long gone. He's a man who's found his second act.

He stands there alone, very still, very powerful, the fake cement running down him like lava, evoking a world of movies of varying degrees of cheapness and popularity: *The Incredible Hulk*, *Swamp Thing*, *Hell Boy*, and no doubt a lot of others that I've never heard of. This, I'm told, is perfectly intentional. It's playfully, knowingly self-referential: it's a homage. The kids love this stuff. But here's the twist. While Motorhead Phil is pulling himself together, shaking off the effects of the explosion, he's suddenly attacked from all sides by velociraptors, swarms of them, a pack, a horde, an exaltation, a murder. He's doomed. It won't end well. Or quickly.

Of course we won't see all of this today. We won't see very much of anything. But we will, at least, sooner or later, see the car being filled. That, at least is being done for real, in real time, here on the sound stage. The explosion will be done later, elsewhere, using a scaled-down model. Then it will be computer enhanced. Then the shots of Motorhead Phil will be cut in. Then the velociraptors will be digitally inserted. What we're watching here and now is a necessary part of the process, but in truth, at least when you've been standing around for half a day, it certainly doesn't seem like the most interesting part.

I've come back to California by myself. Again Caroline decided not to come, and I didn't try to persuade her. She said she'd feel like a gatecrasher, and she had a point. I feel much like a gatecrasher myself, even though without me there'd be no party at all.

There's been idle talk that some later scenes may be shot on a beach in Baja, in Mexico, where the living is easy and the union regulations lax. There's a trailer park down there they could use. How this would fit in with what's already been shot in Fontinella I have no idea. But if it happens then we'll all go down there and perhaps Caroline will join me at last; or perhaps she won't. I find myself vaguely wondering what Josh Martin would have thought about the movie being shot in Mexico, but in general I've stopped wondering what Josh Martin would think about anything.

Beside me on the sound stage, watching events, or non-events, are Leezza and Barry. They are together, happy together, a couple, an item, a partnership, a love thing. Who'd have thought it? Well, lots of people probably, the sort of people who understand the human heart a little differently from the way I do, the sort of people who like happy endings.

It turns out Leezza wasn't trying to kill Barry after all. She was trying to *motivate* him, trying to give him an incentive to lose weight, to encourage him to get out of his car, to do something with his life. Having sex with me all over her Beetle while forcing Barry to watch was part of the same battle plan. Go figure, as they say. It worked too, I suppose.

Leezza is now employed on the movie as a stunt driver, a good career move for her, and the kind of obvious, sensible use of resources that might even have occurred to Josh Martin. And Barry? Well, Barry has indeed been losing weight, effectively and decisively, but under medical supervision so as to ensure that it's not too much too fast. He looks better: how could he not? He's got a long way to go, no doubt, but he's cleaned up his act, cleaned up himself. At least he's moving around now, walking, driving, getting back to his own self, whatever the hell that was.

He now turns to me with a warmth and friendliness I find surprising, considering all that's happened between us, and says, 'So, Ian, is this the way you imagined it?'

If you hear a screaming that comes across the sky, across the tarmac, across the speedway or the sound stage, you shouldn't worry. It's probably not a flying bomb. It's probably not heralding an explosion. The chances are it's just the engine of a Volkswagen Beetle being stressed to breaking point, being thrashed to within an inch of its air-cooled life. Alternatively it may be the sound of the poor author trying to express himself.

# A VEEDUB GLOSSARY
## (in not quite alphabetical order)

**Beetle:** the most common name in English for the Type 1 Volkswagen saloon and convertible, made between 1948 and 2003.

Also sometimes called the Bug, a more common usage in the US than in Britain. I've met people who insist there's a taxonomic distinction to be made between a Beetle and a Bug, but their attempts at explaining the difference have left me none the wiser.

Incidentally, 'Beetle' was a nickname invented and embraced by the general public and actually taken on as a model name by Volkswagen in 1967. Is there any other example of a motor manufacturer responding in this way?

Many countries in the world have also chosen similar nicknames beginning with B: in Croatia the Buba; in Denmark the Bobble; in the Czech Republic the Brouk: in Romania the Brosco.

Others have taken different linguistic routes. Pakistan has gone for the Martiny; in the Philippines it's the Kotseng Kuba, literally the hunchback car; in Israel it's apparently known as the Hiposhit, which I thought was just a silly joke, and it probably is, but even so it seems to be quite a widespread one. And my favourite, if some sources are to be believed, and

I'm not absolutely sure they are, comes from Finland where apparently the Beetle is known as Hitlerin Kosta; Hitler's Revenge.

*'So what do you call that thing?'*
*'A Boby.'*
*'You're from Paraguay, right?'*

**Baja:** literally 'lower' in Spanish, referring here to a type of Beetle modified for use in Baja California, a long peninsula of land in far-western Mexico, directly below the American state of California. The territory is mostly rugged desert, and the scene of gruelling off-road races such as the Baja 500 and 1000. Baja Beetles are raised up, given heavy-duty suspension, big wheels and tyres. The wings and front and rear aprons are reduced or sawn off to accommodate the changes, and the rear deck lid is removed to leave the engine exposed.

**Cal-Look:** Abbreviation of 'California Look', a style of Beetle-customising originating in Southern California and spreading worldwide. Some sources date it back to the 1950s, and it continues to this day, but the 1980s seem to have been its heyday.

Typically a Cal-Look Beetle has been lowered, dechromed, had its bumpers removed, occasionally chopped, channelled and frenched, often with non-standard replacement wheels, preferably from a Porsche. The aim is to create a sleeker, more stream-lined object. Paintwork tends to be ultra smooth and glossy, in primary colours, sometimes two-tone.

Resto-Cal is a less radical version of the look, retaining the integrity of the original car, and some-times going overboard on period accessories.

(The terms lowered, chopped, channelled and frenched can be found in any basic book on car-customising.)

*'Man, that shocking pink Beetle of yours would really look the business in Malibu, but don't you think it might be a bit Cal-Look for Doncaster?'*

**Dune Buggy:** a kind of recreational, Beetle-based kit car. The original body is removed and replaced with a lightweight, open, fibreglass shell. Usually more at home on the beach than in the serious sand-dunes, though Charles Manson was a big fan.

*'So, Chas, do you really think we can fight the Apocalypse in a bunch of clapped-out dune buggies?'*

*'Helter skelter, bitch.'*

**KdF-Wagen:** Kraft durch Freude Wagen, in German literally the 'Strength-through-Joy Car', the original form of the Beetle in Nazi Germany.

*'Hey, Fritz, can you really afford to pay in full, in advance, for a KdF-Wagen that you still don't have a delivery date for?'*

*'It's a struggle, I admit.'*

**Kubelwagen:** literally German for 'Bucket Car', also sometimes Kubel, Kubelsitz, Kubelsitzer, the name of the military 'jeep' style conversion based on the prewar KdF-Wagen and used in World War II. The bodywork was made by a coachbuilder called, I just love this, Trutz of Gotha.

**Nerf Bar:** 'nerf' is US slang for low-impact crash, equivalent to the English 'prang', so a nerf bar was originally a piece of tubular metal, found on old-style racing cars in the States, there as protection during side-on collisions. Today they're found on all sorts of sports vehicles, and on off-road Beetles they sometimes replace the front and rear bumpers.

*'Me, I don't worry about a little nerf now that I've got my nerf bars.'*

**Rat Rod:** form of customised hot rod, not necessarily a Beetle, that has the look of an unrestored or unfinished car. Bodywork tends to be battered, or rusted, or in some cases partially absent.

Fans claim it's a triumph of function over form, but in fact the rat rod has an aesthetic that's as clearly defined as any other design form.

*'Hey, man, that rod looks really rad. Or do I mean rat?'*

*'Whatever.'*

**Sandrail:** a more serious dune buggy or off-road vehicle, often with no body whatsoever but just a tubular roll cage, and a deeply forgiving suspension that allows it to go airborne as it goes over sanddunes and lands spectacularly on the other side.

**Street Sleeper:** a car that on the surface looks ordinary, or less than ordinary, but beneath the humble exterior has mechanics that deliver awesome performance.

*'Hey, mate, why'd you drive a street sleeper?'*

*'Allegory, innit?'*

**Schwimmwagen:** the Type 166, the amphibious form of the Kubelwagen, able to operate in and on water, with a modified crankshaft that can be disengaged from the rear wheels and connected to a propeller.

**Tranny:** slang for transmission, aka gear box.

**Zwitterkafer:** literally in German 'Hermaphrodite beetle', though with the sense of having two uses or being constructed from two different things. The term describes Beetles built in late 1952 and early 1953, with parts from the old Split-Window Beetle, alongside those from the newer Oval. Might also refer to a Beetle driven by an English novelist dressed in women's clothing.

*'What's with the tranny in that Zwitterkafer?'*

# Also by Ian Blackwater

**The Phallicist**
Bob Pettit is an average man: average height, average weight, with an average income, average job and a perfectly averagely sized penis. However, like all men, he certainly wishes he had a little extra in the phallus department.

And then one day his wish starts to come true. His penis begins to get larger, pleasingly at first, then exponentially, then monstrously. He ceases to be a man with a penis and becomes a penis with a man attached.

A savage satire on male desire, potency and inadequacy, and a timely warning about getting too much of what we want. Based on a true story.

**Letters to Thurston**
The year is 1982 and in a boring northern town sixteen-year-old Steve Sterling, sits in his bedroom, practises electric guitar, and listens to the first Sonic Youth album. The music speaks to him and he sends a fan letter to guitarist Thurston Moore, expressing his love of the band and letting out all his personal teenage angst.

Over the years his life progresses – college, drug experimentation, first love, a job, a failed marriage, the death of all his hopes and dreams. And at each crucial stage there's a Sonic Youth album that seems uncannily to match his situation. With each new release he sends Thurston Moore a further confessional letter.

Now as his life spins out of control he decides he must journey to America, track down Thurston Moore, talk to him face to face. Naturally he takes his electric guitar with him. But will it end in an avant-garde free-jazz noise jam or in tragedy?

A bittersweet meditation on the nature of music, mortality and unrequited fandom.


### The Million-Martini Lunch

Part memoir, part travelogue, in which Ian Blackwater scours the world – New York, Sarajevo, Alice Springs, to name but a few – in search of the perfect martini.

He starts at Julio Richelieu's saloon in Martinez, California, where the drink was invented in the late nineteenth century (or was it?). And he goes on to limn the history, the fascination and multiple meanings of the drink sometimes called the silver bullet.

A protean meditation on what we drink, why we drink and what it tells us about who we are. Blackwater discovers some startling and disturbing truths about the martini – and himself!


### Beetamorphosis

'Greg Wintergreen woke from uneasy dreams to find himself transformed into a giant Volkswagen Beetle . . . '

So begins this artful, yet playful, pastiche of Kafka's great work.

A brilliant *jeu d'esprit* and a long-awaited follow-up to Ian Blackwater's cult hit novel *Volkswagens and Velociraptors*.

\*

*Available at all good bookstores, and in some pretty crappy ones too.*